“Do you have time t

“I always have time for my favorite reporter,” Josh said.

Whitney felt a frisson of energy zing up her spine. Of all the new folks, this was the only person whose teasing set her on edge and sometimes made her tremble like dry autumn leaves in a gale.

“Mind if I ask you a question first?” Josh said amiably. “Sort of turnabout’s fair play?”

“I guess not. I have a whole list for you.”

He rested his elbows on the table, leaned forward and studied her for a moment. “Why do you wear those glasses instead of contacts?”

She noticed that he was no longer grinning like a Cheshire cat, so she made a face at him. “That’s a silly question. I need them to read.”

“To read? Or as a mask to hide behind?” he asked quietly.

The Heart of Main Street: They’re rebuilding the town one step—and heart—at a time.

Love in Bloom by Arlene James
July 2013

The Bachelor Baker by Carolyne Aarsen
August 2013

The Boss’s Bride by Brenda Minton
September 2013

Storybook Romance by Lissa Manley
October 2013

Tail of Two Hearts by Charlotte Carter
November 2013

Cozy Christmas by Valerie Hansen
December 2013

Books by Valerie Hansen

Love Inspired

The Perfect Couple
Second Chances
Love One Another
Blessings of the Heart
Samantha's Gift
Everlasting Love
The Hamilton Heir
A Treasure of the Heart
Healing the Boss's Heart
Cozy Christmas

Love Inspired Historical

Frontier Courtship
Wilderness Courtship
High Plains Bride
The Doctor's Newfound Family
Rescuing the Heiress

Love Inspired Suspense

Her Brother's Keeper
Out of the Depths
Deadly Payoff
Shadow of Turning
Hidden in the Wall
Nowhere to Run
No Alibi
My Deadly Valentine
"Dangerous Admirer"
Face of Danger
†Nightwatch
The Rookie's Assignment
†Threat of Darkness
†Standing Guard
Explosive Secrets

*Serenity, Arkansas
†The Defenders

VALERIE HANSEN

was thirty when she awoke to the presence of the Lord in her life and turned to Jesus. In the years that followed, she worked with young children, both in church and secular environments. She also raised a family of her own and played foster mother to a wide assortment of furred and feathered critters.

Married to her high school sweetheart, she now lives in an old farmhouse she and her husband renovated with their own hands. She loves to hike the wooded hills behind the house and reflect on the marvelous turn her life has taken. Not only is she privileged to reside among the loving, accepting folks in the breathtakingly beautiful Ozark mountains of Arkansas, she also gets to share her personal faith by telling the stories of her heart for all the Love Inspired Books lines.

Life doesn't get much better than that!

Cozy Christmas

Valerie Hansen

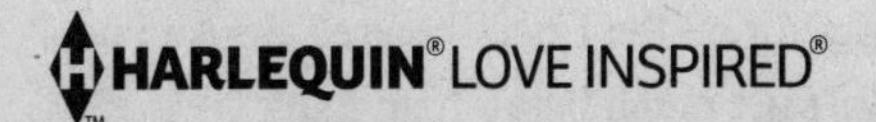

Special thanks and acknowledgment are given to Valerie Hansen for her contribution to The Heart of Main Street miniseries.

Recycling programs for this product may not exist in your area.

ISBN-13: 978-0-373-87853-6

COZY CHRISTMAS

This edition published by arrangement with Love Inspired Books.

www.Harlequin.com

Printed in U.S.A.

Behold, a virgin shall be with child, and shall
bring forth a son, and they shall call his name Immanuel.
—*Matthew* 1:23

To my husband, Joe, and friend, Karen,
who faithfully read and proof for me.
Any remaining mistakes we plan to blame
on someone else. And many thanks to
Shelley Winchester of the Awesome Coffee Cafe in
Salem, AR, for introducing me to the coffee business.

Chapter One

Whitney Leigh rolled her eyes. "Romance! It's getting to be an epidemic."

Because she was alone in the car she didn't try to temper her frustration. Fortunately, the editor of the *Bygones Gazette* had instructed her to use a different approach this time. He wanted her to praise the progress of the stores involved in the Save Our Streets redevelopment project to commemorate their sixth-month anniversary. If he had asked her for one more fluff piece about all the engagements, and even a recent marriage, involving those new businesses, she would have screamed. Just thinking about it made her want to.

Parking in front of the Cozy Cup Café and pausing behind the wheel of her vintage, yellow Mustang convertible, she shivered. A warm, wool coat, scarf and gloves were not enough to make up for the lack of insulation provided by the cloth-topped car. Although it was dear to her heart, there was a lot to be said for a thick, solid roof during the winter, particularly in Kansas.

She pulled the ignition key, set the brake and slid out. Myriad Christmas lights twinkled around nearby shop windows and hung from the colorful awnings that fronted the block of renovated stores.

The Save Our Streets merchants' decorating committee had wound garlands of holly, tinsel and shiny ornaments around the old-fashioned-looking light standards and topped them with banners heralding the holiday season. Coordinated wreaths decked every store entrance while bouquets of silk poinsettias had replaced real flowers around the bases of the evergreens in the quaint planters along the refurbished street. The whole effect was charming. Welcoming.

However, it was also freezing outside. Whitney leaned in to grab her tote bag, slammed the car door and picked her way cautiously through the dusting of fresh snow toward her current assignment.

As a lifelong citizen of Bygones she was supposed to have been perfect for the job of ferreting out the hidden facts concerning the town's mysterious windfall. Too bad she had failed. Instead of an exposé, she'd ended up filling her column with news of people's love lives, when what she needed were reasonable, definitive answers to her more serious queries. But she was not going to quit investigating. No, sir. Not until she'd uncovered the real facts. Especially the name of Bygones's secret benefactor.

A few things were already known, not that that helped much. First, a mysterious philanthropist had bought a whole block of empty buildings on Main Street, then bankrolled a group of merchants from other places to open new businesses in every available location except the old movie house. *Only outsiders could apply.*

"What was *that* all about?" Whitney murmured to herself. Some former shopkeepers had fled when Bygones had started to die but that didn't mean there were no other folks capable of stepping in. If some wealthy person had really wanted to help the town recover and survive after the disastrous downturn in the economy and the permanent closing of Randall Manufacturing, the least he—or she—could have done was relegate the grant money to locals.

The legal arrangement had included them as employees, yes, but never as bosses. That point, alone, was enough to convince her that the anonymous benefactor was not from a small town. He or she obviously had no earthly idea how the minds of country people worked—or how they looked after their own.

She slipped and slid the last yard to the Cozy Cup Café, used the door handle to regain her balance, stepped inside and wiped her boots on the mat, stomping off globs of wet snow as she admired the delicate wreath that hung just inside the glass door. It wasn't the customary green and red colors. Instead, it had been fashioned of brass and gold ribbons and ornaments with snowy accents that perfectly picked up the mocha and cream motif of the shop.

And speaking of coffee… Hearty aromas of freshly ground beans and warm drinks like cider and hot chocolate, as well as the shop's trademark specialty brews, washed over her. If she had not been worried that the handsome barista greeting her with a smile would misinterpret her overt expression of bliss, she might have sighed audibly.

"Cold out there?" Josh Smith asked Whitney.

"Not as cold as it will be in another month." She removed her teal-blue gloves and matching scarf and dropped them into the tote, then began to unbutton her cream-colored coat.

"What can I do for you?"

Whitney was tempted to launch right into her real reason for being there. Instead, she merely said, "Fix me something warm?"

"Like what?"

"Surprise me."

Judging by his lazy smile and the twinkle in his greenish-hazel eyes, she decided she had made a mistake by giving him too much leeway so she added, "As long as it's mostly chocolate."

"Picky, picky, picky."

She couldn't help smiling in return as she settled herself at one of the small, round, glass-topped tables and hung her coat over the back of the wrought-iron chair. There was something unique about this place. And, truth to tell, the same went for the other new businesses on Main. Each one had filled a need and become an integral part of Bygones in a mere five or six months. That, alone, was amazing, particularly given the townspeople's original negative reaction to the so-called invasion.

Josh Smith was a prime example. He was what she considered young—twenty-eight to her twenty-five, according to his original business application—yet he had quickly won over the older generations as well as the younger ones. Some of the retired citizens had begun to make his shop their go-to place for morning coffee, gossip and camaraderie, while teens had adopted his internet cafe as if they had been waiting for it all their lives.

Perhaps they had. Josh's computers were state-of-the-art, with game-playing capabilities far beyond anything she had ever seen.

Wearing a brown-and-white-striped apron over jeans and a polo shirt, he stepped out from behind the counter with a steaming cup in one hand and a taller, whipped-cream-topped tumbler in the other.

"Your choice," he said pleasantly, placing both drinks on the table and joining her as if he already knew this was not a social call.

"I see you're not too busy this afternoon. Do you have time to talk?" She reached into her tote for her digital recorder, notepad and a pen.

"I always have time for my favorite reporter," he said.

"How many reporters do you know?" She took a cautious sip from the cup, holding it in both hands to warm her icy fingers.

"Hmm, let's see." A widening grin made his eyes sparkle. "One."

Whitney felt a frisson of energy zing up her spine. Of all the new folks, he was the only person whose teasing set her on edge and sometimes made her tremble like dry autumn leaves in a gale.

Trying to mask her nervousness she put down her cup and tucked stray strands of blond hair behind her ears before donning her glasses and picking up the pen.

"Mind if I ask you a question first?" Josh said amiably. "Sort of turnabout's fair play?"

"I guess not. I have a whole list for you."

He rested his elbows on the table, leaned forward and studied her for a moment. "Why do you wear those glasses instead of contacts?"

"What?"

"Those clunky glasses. The heavy frames."

She noticed that he was no longer grinning like a Cheshire cat so she made a face at him. "That's a silly question. I need them to read."

"To read? Or as a mask to hide behind?" he asked quietly. "You have beautiful green eyes but I have to really work to see them clearly behind those lenses."

"Why would you want to?" Whitney asked before she realized she might not want to hear his answer. Instead of waiting, she waved her hands as if erasing a chalkboard and added, "Never mind. Forget it. There's already an epidemic in this crazy town and I do not intend to let myself catch whatever it is that's going around."

Josh rocked back and raked his fingers through his short, auburn hair before lacing his fingers behind his neck. "You've lost me."

"Romance, engagements, endless talk of marriage,"

Whitney blurted, immediately coloring with embarrassment. "Do you realize that nearly every one of the new shops is the setting for some kind of pairing? It's ridiculous."

"Considering it an illness is not very flattering to the couples involved."

"Listen," Whitney drawled, "you can pooh-pooh it all you want. I don't think it's a bit funny." She thumbed through her notes, found what she was looking for and began to read. "First, there was the florist, Lily Farnsworth, and Tate Bronson. They're already married. Then Melissa Sweeney at the bakery took up with her own Mr. Cupcake, Brian Montclair. They're getting married next month."

"Well, yes, but..."

Whitney touched the paper with the tip of her pen. "I'm not through. The hardware store is just as bad. Patrick Fogerty is going to marry Gracie Wilson, providing she doesn't run away and leave him standing at the altar like she did her first groom. And what about Allison True?"

"That one shouldn't count," Josh argued. "Allison and Sam Franklin had a history already. I understand the only reason she was considered for one of the grants to start her bookstore was because she'd been away from Bygones for so many years she was no longer thought of as a local."

"Fine." Whitney sighed and paused for a sip of her mocha latte. "Then explain the pet store romance and engagement."

"You can't include that one, either."

"Why not?"

"Because Vivian Duncan works for Allison, not Chase Rollins. His store had nothing to do with it."

Looking past him and seeing a group of teens entering, Whitney said, "You'd better go. You have customers."

"That bunch?" Josh barely took his eyes off her. "They

just want to play computer games. They can log themselves on without my help."

He rested his chin in his palms and gave her another lazy grin. "So, what was it you wanted to interview *me* about? I'm all yours."

At that moment, all Whitney could think to ask was, *How did you get so good-looking?* She was certainly not going to give voice to anything like that.

Instead, she pushed her glasses up the bridge of her nose with one finger and pretended to concentrate on her notes while she wrestled to subdue her errant emotions. She wished her cheeks didn't feel so unusually warm.

Josh could tell his casual repartee had rattled the cute reporter. Well, too bad. She had been sticking her nose into his business from the moment he'd arrived in Bygones. If she had been old and ugly, or even just a little slow-witted, he'd have been fine. Unfortunately, she was none of those things.

Thinking about his prior encounters with Whitney made him smile. Actually, any time he let his thoughts drift her way he found an unexpected lift. His rational mind kept arguing that there was no good reason for feeling that way, yet he did. And that connection was getting stronger the longer he knew her.

In view of the fact that he still had a successful software business to run in St. Louis, developing an emotional attachment to the local reporter was not only foolish, it was counterproductive. He had never intended to stay past the first of the year and nothing had happened since his initial arrival in Bygones to change those plans. Now that his coffee shop was starting to show a profit he felt certain it would be salable. So why was he starting to have mental reservations about putting it on the market?

"Hey, don't look so depressed," Whitney joked, sounding slightly nervous. "My boss wants me to write about the successes of the new businesses and how being in Bygones has affected their owners. I'm not going to ask you anything I haven't already asked all the other grant recipients."

"Okay. Fire away."

"You once told me you had never run a coffee specialty store before. What made you decide to learn?"

Josh shrugged, hoping he looked nonchalant. "I don't really know. I was kind of a computer buff and I thought the two would go together pretty well. By the time I heard about this opportunity, the bookstore people had decided not to serve coffee there, so I thought I'd try it with my computers. I like espresso and I figured the local kids would take to the games."

"Was it hard to learn how to make the different drinks?"

"Not really. I got a book and watched a tutorial on the internet. After that it was mostly a matter of practicing." He grinned. "I did drink a lot of my own coffee those first few weeks while I experimented."

Whitney glanced at the chocolaty concoction he'd served her. "Well, you certainly have a knack for it. This is delicious."

"Thanks. As long as I stick to a set formula I do fine. The only customers who throw me are the ones who like to invent their own recipes, then expect me to remember and repeat them months later."

"You have plenty of computers here. You could use one to make a special file for each person."

Smart, Josh thought. *Too smart.* "Good idea," he drawled. "I'll have to give that some thought."

"So, tell me more about the other part of your store. When did you get interested in computers?"

"In college," he said, hoping she wouldn't pursue the subject further. "It's just a hobby."

Whitney's brows arched. "A hobby? I heard you had

repaired laptops for friends, plus you keep all the stations in this place working perfectly. That's a little more than a hobby."

"Not necessarily. All it takes is a logical mind."

"Which you obviously have. You mentioned college. Where did you go to school?"

This was getting a bit too personal to suit Josh. "Let's just say I didn't graduate and leave it at that, shall we?"

"Really? That surprises me since you seem so capable. What was your major?"

Standing abruptly, Josh picked up the taller drink and paused next to the table. "Sorry. I have to get back to work," he said, forcing a smile, "and make sure the kids don't download something that's too advanced or adult for them. Enjoy your coffee."

"What do I owe you?" Whitney called, lifting her cup for emphasis.

"No charge. It's on the house."

He could have told her that she owed him a lot more than she knew, but he held back. If things went as planned, he'd never have to reveal his part in the rescue of the struggling little town that was such a nostalgic part of his mother, Susanna's, memories. At least not before he left there for good—and, hopefully, not even then.

He had not launched this recovery project for the accolades it might bring him. He had done it for unselfish reasons, to surprise and please his mother. However, considering the scope of his investment in the captivating Kansas town, he doubted he'd ever tell anyone how much of his personal fortune he had spent on the Save Our Streets project.

Josh huffed. So, Whitney wanted to know how being in Bygones for six months had affected him, did she? The honest answer was, *adversely.* He was actually starting to question the wisdom of his firm, sensible plans to sell out soon and move back to St. Louis.

Spending money to benefit others was not his problem. He simply hoped he had not inadvertently invested too big a part of himself.

Whitney took her time getting into her coat, wrapping the scarf around her neck and pulling on her gloves. Of all the merchants whom she had interviewed, this man was the hardest to understand. To begin with he had seemed a lot like the others, but as she'd gotten to know everyone else she had realized that Josh Smith was different.

Of course, any guy who lived and breathed computers the way he did had to be a little odd. And very intelligent. Perhaps that was why she was having such a hard time drawing him into a revealing conversation.

Watching him bending over one of the work stations in which the teens were engrossed, she shook her head. Truth to tell, she got more usable responses from Pepper, the talking parrot in Chase Rollins's Fluff & Stuff pet shop, than she did from Josh.

Looking up the name Smith on college rolls was an option that was likely to take her forever. And, since he had dropped out, she'd have even less chance of learning anything about his past that way.

For the first time since she'd met him it occurred to her to wonder if Smith was his real name.

Shaking herself, she banished that thought. The SOS—Save Our Streets—committee had vetted each applicant. Coraline Connolly had headed up the process and nobody was going to put anything over on the savvy school principal.

Plus, Miss Coraline was Josh's mentor for the project. There was no way he'd have been able to fool her. Absolutely not.

Waving to him as she deliberately passed close by, she said, "Thanks for the coffee."

He barely glanced at her. "You're welcome. Have a great day."

"Oh, I plan to," Whitney said, hesitating to make sure he was paying attention. "Since you're not able to continue our interview, I think I'll stop over at the school and see if Miss Coraline is too busy to chat."

Josh's head snapped around so quickly she wondered why the action didn't give him whiplash. "Coraline? Why?"

"Because she's the one who got the original letter that started all this new commerce," Whitney said. "Besides, she's the SOS committee member who was paired with you right from the start. I can get her take on the project from the beginning and see how positive she feels about the great progress everyone has made. It'll be perfect background for my article. Bye now."

If Whitney hadn't been so determined to remain professional she might have giggled at his widening gaze and uneasy expression. Clearly, she had touched a nerve. Maybe she'd been going about this investigative reporting job all wrong. Maybe, instead of simply interviewing the newbies, she needed to go farther back. Dig deeper into the origins of the renewal plan. Ask to see the original paperwork instead of merely the copies that Coraline had circulated when she'd called the first town meeting and formed the oversight committee.

Although Josh had turned away from her as she walked to the door, she could still sense his awareness, still feel an inner vibration of the energy that had arisen from their proximity.

That shouldn't surprise me, she admitted ruefully. When that man was around she could not ignore him. Not even a little.

Whitney smiled slightly as she walked back to her car.

It was gratifying to see that Josh Smith was becoming as responsive to her presence as she was to his. Which was one more reason—perhaps the best reason of all—why she needed to know what he was hiding and why he refused to talk about his past.

Chapter Two

The spirit of Christmas was everywhere in Bygones. When Whitney turned onto Bronson Avenue on her way to the school she saw more sparkling decorations festooned with uncountable twinkling lights. Where the snow had melted from passing traffic, the red bricks of the street reflected the flickering above and lent a feeling of warmth to the otherwise wintry scene.

It was late enough in the afternoon for classes to have been dismissed. Coraline Connolly's aging blue sedan, however, was still in the faculty parking lot. From the look of it, it had sat there all day because it was frosted with fluffy snow like a cake dusted with powdered sugar.

Whitney parked her Mustang next to Coraline's car and entered the brick, two-story building. Inside, the halls were decorated with posters announcing a school Christmas program as well as the community caroling and tree-lighting ceremony at the park.

Nostalgia washed over Whitney, carrying her back to the thousands of times she had been in that building as a student. A deep breath brought the familiar odors of the place; a base of wet sneakers, glue, plastic and stale sack lunches overlaid with a hint of cleaning solution. She would have known where she was if she'd arrived there blindfolded.

The heels of her boots ticked a cadence on the polished hallway and echoed off the walls as she hurried toward the principal's office. No matter how many times she came here, she always experienced a surge of memories that made her feel more like a teen than an adult.

Whitney was smiling when she paused at the open door to Coraline's office and rapped on the jamb. "Good afternoon. Have you got a minute?"

"Of course, dear." Circling her desk, the gray-haired principal opened her arms to her visitor and gave her a motherly hug. "I was meaning to phone you anyway, just hadn't gotten around to it." Her already pleasant smile widened and her blue eyes sparkled. "I need another volunteer to bake three dozen cookies for the tree-lighting ceremony this coming Saturday."

Whitney returned the hug, then stepped back. "Only if you give me permission to buy them from Melissa at the bakery. I don't do a lot of cooking."

"Then how are you ever going to snag yourself a decent husband? Don't you know the way to a man's heart…"

"Is through his stomach," Whitney supplied with a soft laugh. "So I've heard."

"Well then?"

She shook her head so hard she dislodged one end of the scarf loop that circled her neck. "Well, nothing. If I never hear about another supposedly amazing romance, I'll be happy. If you've been reading the *Gazette,* you know my boss has had me covering a bunch of lovey-dovey stuff lately. I've decided it must be some kind of epidemic."

"That is a rather negative spin to put on it," the principal observed.

"Now you sound like Josh."

The older woman stared. "You've been talking to Josh Smith?"

"I've been trying to." Whitney plopped into a side chair

and sighed. "That man is harder to interview than anybody I've ever met."

"Probably just the kind of mind he has. You know what I mean. Some people are talkers, like you and I, while others are deep thinkers, like Josh."

"You're probably right. Which is partly why I'm here," Whitney explained. "I thought it might help if I could take a peek at the legalese that came with the business grants."

"I supplied everyone with copies," Coraline said.

"I know. I have those. I was just wondering if there might be some clue in the originals that wasn't in the packets you handed out."

"A clue to what?"

"The origin of the grants. You know the saying, follow the money."

"Sorry. There's nothing in those papers you haven't already seen." She returned to the chair behind her desk and made herself comfortable. "Is there anything else I can do for you?"

"Outside of telling me the name of Mr. Moneybags, I guess not."

"Mister? Why do you believe it's a man?" Coraline asked. "I think women are far more likely to be philanthropic, don't you? It's our tendency to nurture."

"I suppose you're right. When I first started looking into this for the *Gazette,* I thought of the benefactor as either male or female. Lately, though, I'm starting to see him as a man."

"Whatever you say, Whitney." The principal picked up a pen and sorted through a pile of papers on the desk until she found the one she wanted and brought it forward. "So, can I put you down for three dozen?"

"Yes, ma'am."

"Excellent. If you're coming to the ceremony you can

just drop the cookies off that night. I'll have a table set up next to the hot chocolate the Cozy Cup is providing."

"Josh is bringing enough for the whole *town?*"

Coraline busied herself making notes on the list. "We all pitch in every year. You know that. I'm sure others will donate, too."

"Right. I'd better stop by Sweet Dreams and get those cookies ordered before Melissa's swamped. She says she won't know for sure until she's been in business for the whole year, but she predicts this is going to be her best season."

"I suspect so," Coraline said sweetly. "I'm looking forward to having my children home for the holidays. How are your parents doing?"

"Fine, thanks. I wasn't sure Mom would survive Dad's knee surgery but he's back on his feet and she's stopped doting on him so much."

"You're very fortunate to have such a satisfying life." Her smile faded. "Not all of my former students have been so blessed."

"Maybe that would be a good hook for another series of articles," Whitney ventured, picturing a headline and framing it in the air with her hands. "Teen leaves small town looking for happiness and discovers that he or she had it all the time, right here in Bygones."

Once again, Coraline seemed unduly bothered. Whitney stood and approached the desk. Reverting to her student attitude she asked, "Are you all right, Mrs. Connolly?"

"I'm fine, dear. Just terribly busy. You understand, don't you?"

"Of course."

"Perhaps we can chat more at the tree lighting. A few of our students are going to be wearing elf hats and helping to pass out the goodies. I'll be there to keep an eye on them."

"What about the church? Are they going to bring the crèche down to the park, too?"

"Not this year. They're doing a live drama program called *Bethlehem,* with a real donkey and a few sheep." She smiled. "I suspect it would be best to keep the livestock confined to the churchyard where the rest of the stable is set up."

"You're probably right." Whitney started for the door. "Thanks for your time. Sorry to have bugged you."

"Think nothing of it, dear."

As Whitney left the office she happened to glance back over her shoulder. Coraline was watching. And there was a definite frown wrinkling her brow.

Since the older woman had lived and worked in Bygones all her life, Whitney supposed she did take special events very seriously; she just hated to see the principal looking so unduly burdened.

The small, sparsely furnished apartment over the coffee shop was not up to Josh's usual standards. He had two reasons for occupying it. One, it was foolish to waste money setting up a real home in Bygones when he wasn't planning to stay. And two, he didn't want to give the impression that he could afford better. It had been difficult enough to honestly answer questions about his efforts to spruce up the empty movie theater located next to his shop. Everybody knew it wasn't included in the grants so he'd had to play down his personal investment.

It was the industry-wide shift from 35mm film to digital presentation that had drawn his interest—and had caused the theater's former owner to sell to his dummy corporation so cheaply. The cost of conversion was going to be expensive and might never pay off.

Josh, however, was delighted for a chance to tinker with a computer-driven system. If all went well, he hoped to surprise Bygones by opening with a free showing of a Christmas movie within the month.

Personally, he didn't see why practically everybody got so sentimental at this time of year. As his father had often said while entertaining business associates in their palatial home, emotional attachments to tradition were nothing but useful tools.

The late Bruce Barton had paid professionals to decorate his home and office for the lavish holiday parties he'd hosted, relegating Josh's mother, Susanna, to the task of playing glamorous hostess. Every time Susanna had tried to add homey touches to the austere but elegant decorations, Bruce had made fun of her efforts and insisted she remove them. By the time Josh was a young teen, she had stopped trying and had meekly complied with whatever made her husband happy.

Josh suddenly felt compelled to phone his mother. It was because of her that he'd begun the Bygones rescue project, although she didn't know it. She was the one with nostalgic memories of the town, not him.

She answered on the second ring. "Hello?"

"Hey, Mom. I tried to connect with you by computer a couple of times. You must have the instant messaging feature turned off."

"Josh! It's wonderful to hear your voice." She sniffled, making him wonder if she was catching cold. "You know computers hate me. The whole system shut down about a week ago and refuses to work. I suppose I'll have to call one of your techie friends to have a look at it—unless you're planning on coming home soon."

"I've been pretty busy," he said, wishing he could tell her the whole truth about his absence right now, instead of waiting.

"Well, just so you won't have to worry about me during the holidays, I'm going on a Caribbean cruise with two other widows. We're leaving next week."

That made sense. After all, she was alone now and must be knocking around in that big house his father had insisted upon. Why she didn't sell it and truly move on was beyond him.

"That's a good first step," Josh told her. "If there's Wi-Fi on the ship you can keep me posted about all the fun you're having."

"I suppose so," Susanna replied softly. "I miss you, honey."

"I miss you, too. We'll get together and catch up on everything after you come home all tanned and relaxed."

"I'm surprised it's taking you so long to set up that new branch of Barton Technologies."

Josh had almost forgotten his necessary cover story. "I should be done by the first of the year."

That much was true. Actually, he could have left Bygones months ago and been assured that his money was being well spent. So what had kept him?

The notion that he might be starting to like his life in the small town was too ridiculous to consider seriously. He was completing a necessary job, that's all. He might not be creating the computer software design administrative center that his mother imagined, but he was still working. And he was pretty proud of the results he was seeing.

Main Street had recovered beyond his wildest dreams. Merchants and the Save Our Streets committee had worked together to produce a model shopping area that was not only appealing, it was also profitable. Even his coffee specialty shop and computer gaming business was showing a slight gain, and it was just a front for his real occupation as a cutting-edge software designer and founder of Barton Technologies.

There were times when Josh felt like one of those comic

book superhero characters, with a mild-mannered facade hiding extraordinary powers.

Grinning at the inane image, he told his mother, "If your computer would boot up, I could fix it from here. Since it won't, I'll send somebody over before you leave for your cruise. How about tomorrow?"

"That's fine," Susanna said. "Love you."

"Me, too," he mumbled, returning to the reticence he had learned so well while growing up. "Bye."

Affection was rarely shown and even less often spoken of during his childhood. That was simply the way it was. Only after his father's death had his mother begun to tell him she loved him. It was still difficult to echo her sentiment in spite of the fact that Josh loved her dearly.

He ended the call, stared at the phone for a few seconds, then shoved it back into his pocket and sat down at one of his computers to email the Barton tech support team.

As Whitney entered Melissa Sweeney's Sweet Dreams Bakery, she couldn't repress a grin. Seeing macho Brian Montclair behind the counter with his blondish hair and sporting a holiday-themed apron was just too funny. The guy was built like a linebacker, yet he'd managed to fit into this job. Finally. Getting rid of the chip on his shoulder over not getting a chance to start a repair garage had taken some doing. Of course, romancing his boss hadn't hurt, either.

"Hey, Brian," Whitney said. "I need to place a rush cookie order."

"Sure thing. Melissa's already got a bunch of those stacked up. What do you need and when?"

"Late Saturday afternoon. About three dozen. I'll make it easy for her and just take whatever kind she bakes. They're for the tree-lighting ceremony in the park."

"Gotcha." He was painstakingly making note of her order. "You still poking into the secret Santa deal?"

"If you mean looking for the mysterious money man, yes. Why? Do you know who it is?"

"Nope. But Melissa got another one of those pep talk messages in the mail. I figure the others did, too."

"Interesting. Mind if I have a look at yours?"

"Not at all." He reached behind him to a ribbon where his boss—and fiancée—had hung a string of Christmas cards, and plucked one from the group. "Here you go. Short and sweet."

"Rats. It's printed, just like before. I was hoping to see a handwriting sample this time."

"Guess the guy's too smart for that," Brian offered.

"Do you think it's a man, too? I didn't at first, but I'm starting to lean that way now." Whitney handed the card back to him.

"Yeah, I do," the former mechanic said. "I guess it's because of the way he operates. You know. Using plain stationery at first, now that card. Compared to the frilly way Lily designed all the Christmas decorations and the fancy cakes Melissa makes, that's barely even a holiday greeting, let alone girly."

Pensive, Melissa studied the card as he hung it back up. "You're right. It not only looks masculine, it's generic. Not even very festive. I suppose it could have been chosen just to throw us all off but it does make me wonder."

"Anything else I can get you?" he asked.

"Um. I'd love to take home half the goodies in your cases but I just had a mocha latte at the Cozy Cup so I'd better not."

She started for the door as new customers entered. Waving, she called, "I'll be back for the cookies after three on Saturday. Okay?"

Brian's nod and smile was all the answer she needed.

That plain greeting card *was* a clue. It had to be. And

if all the other new businesses had received identical messages, maybe she'd be able to trace their origin.

Chances of doing so were slim to none, yet, at this point, Whitney was ready to try anything. Her next move was a visit to each merchant in the heart of Main Street to ask if they had received cards similar to the one at the bakery.

Love in Bloom was right next door. That was where she would begin, walking rather than bothering to move her car out of the lot behind the bakery.

"Plus, I can ask Lily how it feels to have had the first wedding," she muttered, once again recalling the phenomenon of escalating romances. Lily had been the first to succumb. Therefore, if Whitney's next column needed a personal interest touch she could always include more about Tate Bronson's whirlwind courtship of the pretty florist.

Besides, she added, this was going to be his daughter, Isabella's, first Christmas with both a mama and a daddy, so it would lend family interest to the article.

A sense of contentment bathed Whitney as she remembered celebrating Christmas as a child. Rather than there being a specific memory of past holidays, she felt it more as an overall sense of well-being, of love.

Those thoughts brought her directly to the love that God had shown when he'd sent His son into the world so long ago. That was the basis of her love of Christmas. Pleasant family experiences merely grew from the core of her heavenly Father's amazing gift.

Reaching the door to the flower shop she paused to send a silent "Thank You, God," into the wintry sky.

In the deep reaches of her subconscious there was a stirring of another sentiment. Another reason to give thanks.

As she probed her thoughts, an image appeared. It was the smiling face of Josh Smith.

Chapter Three

Josh was torn between phoning Coraline to try to learn what Whitney was up to and leaving well enough alone. Given the determination of the cute reporter and her parting comment about visiting his Save Our Streets mentor, he decided to place the call. What was the worst that could happen?

"She could figure out who I am," he muttered. He could have disclosed his real name and purpose for coming to Bygones long ago, but once he did so he knew his comfortable niche in the community would disappear. He'd had enough experiences with prior efforts at philanthropy to know that there was no way to remain disengaged without hiding his true identity. No matter how hard people tried to treat him fairly, his money made a difference. A detrimental difference in too many cases.

Coraline's phone rang seven times before an answering machine took the call. Okay. So much for picking her brain. He'd just have to ask a few of the other merchants if Whitney had been snooping around and what, if anything, she had said about ferreting out the secrets behind the grant.

Matt Garman, the teenager whom he'd hired for afternoons so he could work on his programming without being interrupted, had reported on time and was already busy behind the counter filling drink orders.

The poor kid's widowed father was a missionary in Turkey, so Matt lived with his grandparents, pastor Hugh Garman and his wife, Wendy. Giving the kid a job at the Cozy Cup Café had definitely helped Matt become more social. Josh could see a lot of his younger self in the tall, shy sixteen-year-old.

"Matt, you hold down the fort," he said cheerfully as he shed his apron. "I've got a few errands to run. Call my cell if you need anything."

"Yes, sir, Mr. Smith."

Pulling on his leather bomber jacket, Josh smiled. Hearing himself called *Smith* instead of *Barton* still startled him occasionally. By the time he sold the Cozy Cup and returned to St. Louis full-time, he wondered if he'd react the same way when someone at Barton Technologies used his real name?

He turned up his collar the minute he stepped outside. Wind was howling. Holiday banners flapped from the lampposts. The decorations were way too flamboyant for his tastes but he'd stayed silent when the merchants had voted to let Lily design and implement the holiday theme so the street's décor would be coordinated.

Josh had to agree with his father in that respect. The minimalist approach appealed to his senses more. He'd grown up with the perfect, white, conical tree decorated with strategically placed red ornaments and little else other than a matching door wreath. Anything more seemed way over the top.

Pausing in front of the flower shop he stomped clinging, wet snow off his boots before he entered. He had thought his shop was overly festooned until he saw what she had done with her own. The Christmas motif was not only occupying every available space on her display shelves, she had draped so many streamers and so much tinsel from the ceiling he had to fight the urge to duck.

"Hi, neighbor," Lily called, able to see his reflection in the curved mirror she'd rigged between the display area and her workroom. "What's up? I just got in some live poinsettia plants but if you take them out in this weather they'll have to be wrapped well or they'll go into shock and die for sure."

"I'm good on decorations," Josh assured her, wondering where she thought he'd find room for one more unnecessary thing in his already cramped store.

He sauntered around the edge of the counter and into her work space. "I just wondered if you'd had a visit from Whitney. She's been bugging me about our grants again."

Lily nodded and smiled. "She was here. Last I saw of her she was headed down the street, acting like she was on a mission."

"That's normal. What did she say to you?"

Lily laughed. "What *didn't* she say? She is one determined lady when it comes to her job. Apparently, she saw a Christmas greeting from our benefactor at the bakery and wanted to see if I got the same one."

"You showed her?"

"Sure. I'm keeping all my cards as mementos of my first year in Bygones. I may eventually make a scrapbook. I've just been too busy so far."

"Which is a good problem to have," Josh observed. "I saw the special arrangement you made for the church last Sunday. Very impressive."

"Thanks. It's one of the ways I thank God for bringing me here and helping me find the perfect husband." She was grinning broadly. "Which reminds me. Tate wanted me to ask you if you have time to fix his home computer. We're not looking for a handout. He'll be glad to pay."

"That's not necessary," Josh assured her. "Like I always say, it's just a hobby."

"Okay, but if you change your mind..."

"Have him drop it by the Cozy Cup anytime." He had started backing toward the door. "And speaking of business, I'd better get back to mine."

"Watch your step. It's slippery out there."

With a casual wave, Josh strode to her door and stepped outside. He looked up and down the street. No sign of Whitney. He checked his cell, saw no new text messages and turned toward the hardware store. At least it and the pet shop beyond had male proprietors. Their take on Whitney's queries might be more logical than that of the women involved.

Then, if his gut was still tied in knots after talking to Patrick and Chase, he'd stop in at Allison True's bookstore on his way back to work. Whitney Leigh wasn't the only person who could be tenacious.

It seemed odd to Whitney that each shopkeeper, no matter what their wares, had received an identical greeting card. The letters of encouragement in the past had been more detailed, more personally suitable. These cards were nonspecific to the point of being almost insulting.

She handed Allison's back and shook her head. "Thanks. That didn't help at all."

"I was afraid it wouldn't. Sam said the same thing."

Allison's reference to her rekindled romance with high school math teacher and coach, Sam Franklin, set Whitney's teeth on edge. There was no escape. She felt as if she was trapped in a snow globe made up of the perfect little town and its perfect, tiny residents. If she hadn't feared being thought of as callous she might have quoted a famous Dickens character and said, "Bah! Humbug!"

When Allison turned to replace the card in the basket

she was using to collect them, Whitney almost burst out laughing. The slogan printed on the back of her T-shirt echoed those exact words.

"Love your shirt," Whitney said with a chuckle. "It fits my mood perfectly after spending the afternoon chasing down clues and coming up empty-handed."

"Maybe I have something else that will help," the dark-haired woman offered. She reached into the bottom of the basket and produced an empty envelope. "I saved this."

"What is it?"

"There's no return address but the postmark is St. Louis, Missouri. That's where the card came from."

"Really?" Whitney snatched it from her so she could closely examine it. "I wonder if anyone else saved theirs."

"I doubt it. I'm kind of funny that way. I hate to throw things away until I'm sure I don't need them." She giggled. "I still have an old photo of Sam that his sister, Lori, took when she and I were teenagers."

Sam again. Romance again. Whitney rolled her eyes before thinking, happy to note that Allison had apparently not noticed.

"Mind if I keep this?" she asked, taking care to school her features and appear professional.

"No. Not at all. I hope it helps you."

"Thanks," Whitney said, tucking the envelope into her tote. "I've been to all the other new businesses but I'm going to go back and ask if any of them saved envelopes like you did, just in case they're not all the same."

"Have fun," the willowy brunette said. "I can see why you'd want to visit Josh again. If I wasn't so in love with my Sam I'd join you."

"I only go there for coffee. And for information," Whitney insisted, "although I sure don't get much of the latter."

It was Allison's turn to roll her eyes. Whitney ignored her. There was only one newcomer not yet spoken for. Josh

Smith. She was well aware of his single status. She was also aware that there was a standoffish quality to his persona that kept others at arm's length. Whether that was true of everyone or mostly applied to the way he related to her was of no importance.

His actions had been clear. He was barely willing to carry on a meaningful conversation with her, let alone open up and share any confidences. As far as Whitney was concerned, that meant he was interesting without being interested. Particularly in her case.

Well, fine. He could be as closemouthed as he pleased. She'd work around his reticence this time, just as she had in the past. His would be the last shop she would recheck, and when she did, she intended to hang around until he at least showed her the greeting card he had received.

Josh saw his nemesis returning—and she looked more determined than ever. That was not a good sign.

"I'll be in the back," he told Matt. "If anyone asks for me, tell them I'm busy."

"But..."

Without waiting to hear what else the teen had to say, Josh ducked into the computer gaming area and passed through it to the back room. It was here that he did his repairs, reserving his upstairs living quarters for the real work that paid his bills—and supported the large staff of Barton Technologies, as well.

When he had first come to Bygones he had tried to design software on the ground floor. Since it was too hard to concentrate when he had to keep stopping to brew fancy coffee drinks, he had eventually left the workshop area to serve as a diversion and moved his serious business to his second-floor apartment.

Listening at the curtained doorway he heard Whitney's voice. "Hi, Matt. How's it going?"

"Good, Ms. Leigh. What can I get for you? We just got

another fresh delivery from the bakery. How about something sweet?"

"No, thanks," she replied, sounding a bit disgruntled. "I was hoping to catch your boss. Have you seen him lately?"

"Um...yes, but he said he was pretty busy."

Josh peeked past the edge of the curtain in the doorway and saw Whitney's face. Her brow was knit, her head cocked to one side as she studied the teenager through those heavy-rimmed glasses of hers.

When she said, "Okay. I'll wait," Josh decided to step forward, show himself and get it over with.

"Looking for me?"

To his surprise and chagrin, the pretty reporter brightened and began to smile. "Yes!"

Josh did his best to appear relaxed and nonchalant as he sauntered toward her. "Well, you've found me. What's up?"

He saw her scanning the shelves behind the counter where he kept his coffee supplies, cups and flavorings. She was apparently not finding whatever she was looking for, because her smile was fading and her expression was growing more and more intense.

"You don't have any Christmas cards displayed."

"No, I don't. By the time the merchants' decorating committee finished, there was barely room to function, let alone do it comfortably. I saw no reason to clutter up the place with more unnecessary paper."

"But you kept your cards, didn't you?" She stepped closer to him and he could feel the increasing tension.

Cards? She was looking for his Christmas cards?

The reason for her quest struck him like a physical blow. Of course! She meant the cards he'd had sent to the other merchants. And *not* to himself.

Feeling like a fool, particularly where the quick-witted reporter was concerned, he thrust his hands into his pockets and struck a casual pose. At least he hoped it was casual, because his gut was churning and he could feel perspiration developing on his forehead.

"I'm not very sentimental," he said flatly.

"You celebrate Christmas, don't you?"

"Of course. I went forward, accepted Pastor Garman's invitation and joined the church."

"I don't mean that. How about customs and childhood remembrances? Didn't your family celebrate with a tree and presents and things like that when you were young?"

Josh decided it was best to explain. Maybe then she'd stop expecting him to produce the nonexistent card.

"My father didn't go in for a lot of sentimental stuff," Josh said. "He preferred to look at Christmas as an opportunity to further his business interests, and my mother abided by his wishes. Putting wrapped gifts under his fancy, decorator tree would have spoiled the artistic effect."

"That is so sad," Whitney said softly, laying her hand gently on his forearm.

The tenderness in her response caught him unawares and gave him the feeling that her empathy could reach all the way into his heart if he let it.

"Not really," Josh insisted, stepping back just enough to escape her tender touch.

She dropped her hand. "You referred to him in the past tense. Is your father living?"

"No. He passed away just over two years ago."

"What about your mother? Are you planning to go home for Christmas or is she coming here to Bygones?"

"Neither," he said soberly. "My mother is wisely going on a cruise with friends. I'm delighted to see her finally making a new life for herself."

"And you have no siblings?"

He couldn't decide where Whitney was going with these questions but since he had already revealed so much he decided he might as well continue. "I was an only child."

"Oh, dear."

Josh huffed. "You don't have to look so solemn, Ms. Leigh. I assure you, I don't need anything beyond my own company to be content—no matter *what* day it is."

Instead of arguing with him the way he had expected her to, she stared. He could see her eyes glistening.

A solitary tear tipped over her lower lashes and slowed as it passed the rim of her glasses.

Whitney whisked it away and smiled, although Josh was certain it was an effort for her to do so. "Well, you've promised to bring hot drinks to the tree-lighting ceremony on Saturday so I guess I'll see you there. Right?"

"Of course."

She held out her hand as if wanting to shake his. What could he do? He accepted her friendly overture.

The moment their fingers touched, however, he felt a surge of emotion that went straight to his heart and sent warmth flowing through and around him as if an invisible blanket now encompassed them both.

His first mistake had been taking her hand. His second was looking directly into her eyes and recognizing their emotional connection.

Time stopped. It was as if they were totally alone in the midst of the coffee shop, even though Matt was currently waiting on another customer.

More moisture sparkled in Whitney's eyes and Josh sensed his own vision beginning to cloud. He was a practical man, just like his father had been. So what in the world was wrong with him? He didn't need anything but his work to be content. He was planning to sell out and leave Bygones soon. His company needed him back in the home office.

Besides, maudlin sentiment was not a part of his makeup. Nor did he need sympathy. He liked his life as it had been. He knew who he was and where he belonged. Period.

Whitney was the first to break contact. Blinking, she turned away and started for the door.

As Josh watched her leave he was struck by a sense of loss beyond anything he had experienced in the past. Common sense had nothing to do with it.

And that was what scared him all the way from the top of his head to his toes.

If he could no longer rely on pure logic to answer his questions and direct his life, what else was there?

Chapter Four

Whitney felt like patting herself on the back as she carried the pink bakery box from her car to the park Saturday evening. It had taken monumental self-control to keep from opening it at home and having just one or two tastes of the goodies within. Knowing herself well, she had refrained from breaking the tape holding the flaps closed. In her opinion, there was no such thing as having only *one* cookie.

Besides, it was the Christmas season. If a girl couldn't break a few diet rules now, when could she?

That thought brought a wide smile, as did the friendly waves of others who were arriving early to set up for the event. Spotting Coraline standing at a long table next to the fence surrounding the snow-blanketed community garden plot, Whitney headed straight for her.

The decorating committee had outdone itself once again. Every tree, whether evergreen or deciduous, was festooned with twinkling lights, apparently powered by the library on one side of the park and Elwood Dill's Everything store on the other. The lights decorating the gazebo where the carolers would soon gather were reflected off the glassy, half-frozen waters of the nearby pond, making the surface glimmer as if glazed with silver and dotted with diamonds.

In the center of the park, between the fallow garden and

the playground, stood a stately fir. Whitney remembered it as being very tall when she was a child but of course she and the tree had both grown since then. The evergreen had been planted long before her birth by descendants of Bygones's founders, Saul and Paul Bronson, whose legendary feud over a woman had led them to finally settle there and let bygones be bygones. Hence the town's unusual name and its motto, Family First.

Coraline greeted her with a wide grin and reached for the bakery box. "Thank you so much, dear. I'm afraid my volunteer elves are planning on eating more than they pass out. We're going to need every spare cookie."

"Well, I didn't nibble," Whitney told her, "but I was tempted. Melissa's place smells so much like Christmas it made me really crave a taste." She scanned the park, noting that daylight was rapidly fading. "Where's the hot cocoa going to be set up?"

"Looking for a certain handsome barista?"

Whitney scowled. "Of course not. I was just wondering if he'd need power and how we'd get it to him."

"Ah, yes. I see."

"Well, I was."

"Whatever you say, dear." Coraline handed Whitney a tray of neatly arranged cookies. "Why don't you put those over there on the end of the second table and stand guard so the kids don't grab them ahead of time?"

"Over there?" Whitney inclined her head to point since she had her hands full.

"Yes," Coraline said sweetly. "Right next to where I told Josh to park his van."

Inching into the park with Matt Garman seated beside him, Josh leaned over the wheel to peer through the frosty windshield. He'd been to Bronson Park often enough, helping with the community garden project and other things, to know where he was going. Still, he didn't want to damage the grass. There wasn't enough snow to make traveling dangerous, just slippery going if he wasn't cautious.

He flashed his headlights on high beam.

"Over there." Matt pointed. "See? By the fence."

"Got it." Josh could see long tables decked with food, and people gathering around them. There was Coraline. And that looked like Melissa and Brian arriving, too.

At the closest end of the line stood an unmistakable figure wearing a familiar coat, scarf and gloves. Whitney Leigh. Josh gritted his teeth. If that nosy reporter was working with Miss Coraline, there was no telling what leading questions she'd feel free to ask before the evening was over.

As he eased the van to a stop at the end of the last table, Josh spoke to Matt. "I'll keep the supplies coming. You'll be in charge of serving."

"Yes, sir."

Josh bailed out and zipped his leather jacket, noting the misty clouds that his warm breath made when he exhaled into the frigid, evening air.

He circled the white van and slid open the door displaying the Cozy Cup Café logo. It was done in two shades of brown with a cup and saucer as the base. Rising from the cup, like wafting aroma, were ribbons of steam that connected here and there to spell out the name of his specialty coffee shop. Since he had designed the graphic himself, via computer, he was particularly proud of it.

Matt waved to Whitney and the others, then got busy setting up a smaller table containing stacks of foam cups and napkins.

Inside the van, Josh had warmers to keep large containers of rich hot chocolate at serving temperature. They weren't going to offer their usual coffee menu, not even regular Kona coffee. It would be impossible to protect it from turning bitter if they brewed it ahead of time, particularly since he didn't have enough special air pots to hold all they'd need.

Because he had done the prep work back at his shop, it only took him a few more minutes to get everything ready. The park was beginning to fill with an amazing number of celebrants; adults and children. Some were standing still and rubbing cold hands together while others, particularly the younger ones, were racing back and forth between the playground area and the cookie tables.

Matt drew cup after cup of cocoa, adding a squirt of whipped cream as he served them. He even made a special effort to hurry over and present a cup to Whitney when he had a spare moment, although Josh did also see him exchange a handful of cookies for the drink.

He was so deep in thought about the enigmatic reporter he failed to notice Matt's approach.

"Excuse me, Mr. Smith?" the young man said, poking his head in the door past the stainless steel warmers.

"Whoa! You startled me. What's wrong? Are we low on something? Do you need more cups? More whipped cream?"

"No, sir. It's the choir. My grandpa's about to pray and start the singing. They're real short of tenors. Would you mind if I sang with them like I do for church?"

What could Josh say? "Of course not. Go. I can handle this by myself for a while. Just come on back when you're done, if you can."

"Thanks!"

The wide, relieved grin on the youth's face gave Josh a really good feeling. He might not be used to this kind of seasonal celebrating, but there were clearly plenty of others who were. Of course, a preacher's grandson would be among them.

Josh slid out of the van and slammed the passenger side door. He'd left his gloves back at the shop and his hands were freezing now that he was fully outside, so he rubbed them together for warmth before stuffing them in his jacket pockets.

A feminine voice at his elbow asked, “Cookie?”

He whirled, expecting Whitney. It was Coraline, instead. “Thanks. I didn’t have time for supper.”

“Well, these aren’t good for you if you don’t eat anything else,” she lectured, adding a smile to prove she was teasing. “Take two. The oatmeal raisin ones should be filling.”

He did as she’d suggested. “Thanks. How much longer before the mayor lights the big tree?”

“Probably a couple of ‘Silent Night’s and a ‘Noel’ or two,” she said, gesturing toward the assembling choir. “Maybe half an hour.”

“Okay. Good to know.” He stomped his feet. “Man, it’s cold out here.”

“It’s not so bad if you keep moving. What were you doing? Hiding in the van?”

“No, ma’am. I was minding the hot cocoa supply while Matt served.”

“Where did he run off to?”

“The church needed a tenor, or so he claimed. I suspect he may have a girlfriend in the group.”

“Probably. He is sixteen.” Coraline was smiling benevolently. “Tell you what. I’ll loan you one of my helpers until Matt gets back.”

“That won’t be necessary…” She was already hurrying away. To Josh’s chagrin, she stopped next to Whitney and began speaking to her. He couldn’t hear their conversation but he did see her put down the plate of cookies and start waving her arms before pivoting to point right at him.

Of all the hundreds of people available in the park that night, Coraline was choosing to send Whitney! If he didn’t know better, he’d suspect some kind of devious, female conspiracy.

* * *

"Are you sure?" Whitney asked her former principal. "I don't think Josh likes me very much."

"Likes, shmikes," Coraline taunted. "The poor guy lost his only helper and once the singing is over he's likely to have so many folks wanting hot drinks again he'll be snowed under." She giggled. "Pun intended. I can't remember the last time Bygones had snow this early in the year."

"I think I was still in high school," Whitney told her. "We got out of class early and ran around on the playground trying to make snowballs out of whatever we could scrape up."

"I remember that day." The older woman was grinning. "Well, what're you waiting for? Go help the helpless, like the Good Book says."

Whitney doubted anyone else had ever thought of Josh Smith as helpless. She certainly didn't. He was so capable, so organized, it was uncanny. Almost scary, if she let herself dwell on it.

Admiring the man's accomplishments wasn't wrong, she reasoned, it was simply unnerving that she was unable to temper her burgeoning appreciation of everything he said and did.

Providing refreshments for an entire town, for instance. In the past, several service clubs and churches had banded together to prepare a couple of large batches of hot cider or cocoa, but it was nothing like Josh's. He was serving the very best he had. And that had raised her opinion of him another notch.

She didn't have to work to greet him with a broad smile. "Reporting for duty. Miss Coraline says you can use some help over here."

"It was nice of her to worry about me but I've got this. Honestly. Once it's set up it's not hard to manage."

"Then I'll just hang around and entertain you while we

wait and see if you need me." The befuddled expression on his handsome face made her laugh. "Don't worry. I promise not to cook."

"Is that a good thing?" he asked.

"Oh, very good. I remember one time, when I was about twelve, I decided to make a special Christmas morning breakfast to surprise my family. After the fire department came, Dad took Mom and me out to eat way up in Manhattan. It was nearly noon by that time. We had to stay out of the house until they cleared it of smoke."

"You're joking, right?"

That question brought more laughter. "Nope. Totally serious. I was trying to bake a coffee cake, hit the wrong button on the range and locked the door on the self-cleaning oven. There was no way to get it open early and that coffee cake was a cinder by the time the system finished its full cycle. Pretty much ruined the baking pan I'd used, too."

She was delighted to see that her true tale had amused the barista. He took his hands out of his pockets, sidled behind her and dramatically blocked access to his van with his body and outstretched arms.

"In that case, maybe it would be best if you just handed out napkins and I did the rest," Josh said with a melodramatic smirk.

"My thoughts, exactly." Whitney loved to tell stories, making her perfect for her chosen profession. The more she mulled over her past Christmases, the more her spirits rose.

"Most of the time, Mom kept me out of the kitchen," she said. "I must admit it was a relief." She slipped off one glove, held out her hand and pointed to a faint scar on her index finger. "This is from the time I was helping slice tomatoes and I didn't know Dad had sharpened Mom's knives."

Josh just shook his head.

"And this one," she added, choosing another small scar,

"is from trying to chop kindling wood at summer camp when I was about eight. That was in my pretend pioneer phase. Only I wanted to be the one out hunting buffalo, not the one staying behind at the covered wagon to bake biscuits."

To her surprise, Josh reached for her hand and cradled it gently. His touch was light, yet Whitney felt the effects of it all the way from the top of her head to her toes.

With the fingers of his opposite hand he traced the scars as if the injuries were fresh and he was seeking to heal them. "Sounds like you were as fearless back then as you are now," he said softly.

Whitney was rendered speechless. She opened her mouth but no sound escaped. The timbre of his voice was low, enthralling, and when he raised his gaze to meet hers she felt shivers dance along her spine. Was she truly fearless? If so, she was selective in her courage because right now, at this precise moment, she felt as if she might keel over in a dead faint.

It was the thought of that kind of embarrassment that brought her to her senses. She pulled her hand from his. Stepped back. Managed a smile, although she was unsure whether it was convincingly constructed or ludicrous.

"Thanks, I think." Pivoting to face the music, she urged him to do the same. "Listen. You can hear Matt's voice. It's beautiful."

When Josh didn't comment she turned back to him and was startled by his strange expression. He was staring, not at the gazebo where the singers were massed, but at her.

The icy night air was so electrified between them, Whitney half expected to see real sparks arcing like the impressive emissions of lightning from a Jacob's ladder in a physics lab.

The park and its occupants faded into the background. The sound of the music drifted away.

Twinkling lights in the trees blurred until they were nothing more than a faint glow.

Whitney saw Josh take a purposeful step toward her. She held her breath, wondering what he was planning to do.

He slowly raised one hand and drew his finger down the side of her cheek as if he were tracing her portrait and needed to outline it perfectly.

She trembled but stood her ground.

Their eyes met. Gazes held.

Josh's quirky, half smile was only for her.

"Matt's voice isn't the only beautiful thing," he whispered. "There's something about you tonight that I've never noticed before. Something very special."

So nervous she could barely think, let alone come off sounding lucid and intelligent, Whitney employed her usual method of self-defense. She resorted to humor.

"Must be the cookies," she quipped. "I am so full of sugar I should be climbing the walls." She offered a playful smile. "Except we're outside and there aren't any. Walls, I mean."

Josh's laugh sounded uneasy, as if he were just as glad as she was to end their extraordinary moment. "In that case, see if you can find me a couple of the same kind you ate, will you? I suspect I may need all the energy I can muster to keep up with the workings of your brain."

"Cookies won't help," Whitney told him with a wide grin. "I may be a lousy cook but I have a mind like a steel trap." She was chuckling. "Of course, there are times when its jaws snap shut for no reason and I forget to reset it."

Josh was shaking his head in the wake of the inane analogy. He turned away and climbed back into the van, ostensibly to check the warmer, leaving Whitney standing alone by the serving table.

Why had she made a silly joke about a very nice compliment? Why was it so hard to accept one coming from

Josh? Was it because their previous encounters had been so fraught with tension? Or could it be because she was starting to like him far too much and realized how little she really knew about him?

Either was possible. Only one had a solution. If he continued to hide his past she would have to start digging deeper and casting a wider net, excuse the clichés.

The hardest part of her plan would be accepting whatever she discovered, when all she really wanted was to return to the moment when he had touched her and relive it, over and over and over.

Chapter Five

Bygones's mayor, Martin Langston, was introduced by Pastor Hugh Garman, Matt's grandfather, as soon as the caroling ended.

Leaning on his cane, Langston took the portable microphone in his free hand and began. "Wonderful music, Reverend." Waiting for the applause of the crowd to die down, he then added, "I've given the signal to light our town tree so many times I suspect I could do it blindfolded, yet every year I find I have the same thoughts when this time comes."

Josh had gotten out of the van and meandered along with the rest of the assemblage, including Whitney, to gather around the gazebo. It pleased him that she didn't seem startled when he leaned closer to her shoulder and asked, "Do I sense a speech?"

"Undoubtedly." Smiling, she gave him a brief glance. "I can just about quote it from memory. But the mayor is sincere and loyal. Considering that he doesn't get paid for all the things he does for this town, I guess he's entitled to grab what little limelight he can."

The rotund, graying mayor's oration was continuing, earning benevolent smiles and nods from his audience. He paused for effect, then concluded with "We must always remember the true reason for Christmas and keep our Savior's birth as the primary focus of our celebration, in spite of enjoying all the other benefits we share, both here, tonight, and in our homes." He harumphed. "And remember, shop in Bygones!"

Josh applauded along with the others. He'd been so caught up in Whitney's nearness he'd missed most of the speech until the end. That part, he definitely agreed with. Being a merchant, even when his store was not his real livelihood, had shown him the importance of seasonal festivities. His net had improved so much lately there was a chance the Cozy Cup Café would actually start to show a decent profit. A profit he had not expected.

Which meant he could soon sell the shop and leave town as planned, without feeling guilty. He certainly didn't want to cheat new owners. He would never misrepresent his success—or lack of it. Of course, whoever took over would need to be pretty good with computers to keep all the stations working. That meant it might be difficult to find just the right buyer.

The thought of actually leaving Bygones struck a blow to his consciousness that took him aback. He had always intended to restore Main Street for his mother's sake, then walk away, so why was that notion suddenly making him edgy? It was as if that perfectly logical plan was no longer suitable.

How could that be? He was a totally rational guy. A man who set his mind on a goal and accomplished it. Which he had done, according to the reports all the other grant recipients had submitted to his auditors via the dummy corporation.

His gaze rested on Whitney, taking in her fair, blond hair and noting the way it draped in silky waves over the bulk of the bluish scarf around her neck. She was short enough that he could have easily rested his chin on the top of her head and wrapped her in a warm embrace. A few other couples, like Vivian Duncan and Chase Rollins, were doing exactly that and looked blissfully happy.

The urge to reach for Whitney was strong. His will to resist was stronger and he stuffed his cold hands back into his jacket pockets.

"Watch the tree," she told Josh, breaking into his thoughts. "Mayor Langston is about to give the signal."

Josh could not have cared less about the tree. All he had eyes for was the woman standing in front of him. The stubborn, unpredictable, intelligent—beautiful—woman.

And since she was clearly unaware of his personal interest, he was going to give himself the gift of indulging it by looking at her.

Whitney's shivers were caused less by the winter temperatures than by her enhanced awareness of the man directly behind her. She imagined she could feel his warm breath tickling her hair. Could he really be that close? Surely not. Her vivid imagination was running amok, that was all. It was time to rein it in. And she would. Soon. Just not quite yet.

The mayor raised his cane and gestured toward the highly decorated tree. "Three…two…one!" He brought the cane down in an arc.

The expected brightness of the Christmas lights gave an added glow to the scene as townspeople oohed, ahhed, cheered and applauded.

Whitney felt her spirits lift and her sense of belonging swell until she was grinning from ear to ear. "Isn't it wonderful? Look how perfectly they've arranged all the lights. Every year it gets prettier."

"I assume you've lived here all your life," Josh said.

"Yes. Born and raised. I understand you're from Missouri."

"How did you know that?"

It amused Whitney to see him scowling and seeming unsettled. "I read it in your business application, of course. How did you think I found out?" She laughed lightly as he continued to give her a perplexed stare. "I may consider myself an investigative reporter but I must admit, you have me mostly stumped."

The frown lines in his forehead relaxed. As far as Whitney was concerned, that proved he had something to hide. Something he didn't want her or anyone else to know.

The first thing that came to mind was the possibility he was some kind of criminal. That silly thought didn't last the length of a heartbeat. No. Josh Smith might be hiding his past for some reason but she was certain he was in no way disreputable. Enigmatic, yes. Evil, no.

She smiled up at him as the crowd around the gazebo began to disperse. "We'd better get back to your van. It looks like we're about to get more customers."

"Right. Can you stay to help until Matt shows up? I'd really appreciate it."

Whitney said, "No problem," aloud while silently vowing to spend the rest of this amazingly wonderful evening with Josh no matter what.

Yes, she was still a reporter at heart. And, yes, she still wanted—needed—to know a lot more about him.

But there's no hurry, she insisted, satisfied to merely enjoy his company for the time being. The attraction she felt for the inscrutable man may have begun with curiosity about his past but it was far more than that by now. She liked him, actually liked him. That opinion was not dependent upon the life he may have once lived. It was based solely on the thrill she felt whenever he smiled at her or spoke her name.

"Uh-oh," Whitney mumbled, acknowledging the depth of her folly as she followed Josh back to the coffee van. No level-headed woman, particularly a savvy newspaper reporter like her, would let herself become enamored of a virtual stranger without being more certain of his history.

Yet there she was, scuffing her way across the trampled grass and packed snow, following a person about whom she knew practically nothing.

Could she trust her instincts? Whitney wondered. Or was she already past the point where being sensible applied?

If she had known the answers to those questions she might have felt a lot better about her errant feelings.

Then again, she mused as she watched Josh striding along ahead of her, where that particular man was concerned she seemed to have little common sense left.

The immediate demands of the crowd left Josh no time in which to consider his attraction to Whitney versus her penchant for digging into his past. By the time the revelers were starting to drift off and return to their respective homes, he had managed to relax considerably. Whitney could not possibly know who he was or why he had come to Bygones. If she'd had even a hint of the truth, she would be peppering him with leading questions.

Therefore, he told himself, his secret was still safe. The question was, should he continue to pretend he was Josh Smith? He knew Whitney would be furious no matter when she learned his true identity. But, because he was starting to care about her opinion, he wondered if it might be advantageous to make an official announcement right before he left for good? Perhaps the grand opening of the old movie house would be a good time.

No. My original strategy is the most sensible course, he concluded easily. He'd thought it all through even before deciding to fund the town. There was no reason to change his mind now and take the chance of ruining a perfectly logical scheme.

However, his musings had reminded him of something he'd been meaning to do.

"Remember how I told you I was tinkering with the projection system in the empty theater next to my shop?" Josh asked Whitney.

"Vaguely. I haven't heard much about it lately. How's it coming?"

"Very well." He slid the folded table into the back of the van with his other supplies and slammed the rear door.

"That's great! Can I include it in my next article about the Main Street merchants?"

"Actually, I was hoping you'd do a separate short feature as promo for the reopening. I thought I'd have a free screening sometime between Christmas and New Year's. What do you think? Would people come then?"

"It's more likely than if you schedule it before Christmas. What film are you planning to show?"

"It's A Wonderful Life."

"Oh, I love that one!"

"A lot of folks do, I guess."

Whitney giggled. "Why am I getting the idea that you're not one of them?"

"Beats me. I like that film better than the ones with Santa Claus in them."

"Because your parents used to fool you about Santa bringing toys down the chimney?"

Josh's brow knit. "No. Actually, I was never taught about Santa or reindeer or elves or any of that stuff." When he saw Whitney's mouth gape he had to laugh. "Well, I wasn't. Of course I never heard much about the *real* Christmas story, either. If my mother had not taken me to Sunday school a few times I might never have heard of Jesus."

"That's terrible."

"Not really. It's hard to miss something you've never

had," Josh said flatly. "As I told you, my dad was a no-nonsense kind of guy."

"What about your mother? She did take you to church?"

"Occasionally. Come to think of it, we went when Dad was out of town on business, so I doubt he even knew, not that he would have cared, other than to insist we were wasting our time."

Josh noticed an added sparkle to Whitney's eyes when she took off her glasses and pocketed them.

"You said your mother was going to be on a cruise at Christmas this year?"

He nodded. "That's right."

"Then why not spend the day at my house, with my family? We'd love to have you join us."

"Thanks, but no thanks. I wouldn't fit in."

"How about some other night then? Unlike me, my mom is a great cook. She has never once come close to setting the kitchen on fire."

"Well, maybe." He shrugged, wondering why he had such a strong urge to accept her offer.

"Tell you what," Whitney said, brightening. "Look for us in church tomorrow morning. I'll introduce you to my family and Mom can invite you herself."

"You really don't have to put yourself out, Whitney." He managed a half smile that lifted one corner of his mouth higher than the other.

"If I didn't want you to come for supper, I wouldn't have asked you in the first place," she countered.

Josh's grin widened. "I know you. You probably think if you can get me into a casual social setting I'll slip and reveal more about myself. Right?"

"Hey, I never claimed my motives were totally above suspicion. Just remember, if I wasn't trying to be neighborly I'd have stuck to trying to trace you via the internet. I don't have to take you home and feed you to research you."

"True enough. What I don't understand is why you feel it's so important to dig into my private life. Believe me, I'm just a regular guy."

When Whitney sobered and said, "There is nothing regular about you," Josh was stunned. Once again, she was sounding as if she knew more about him than she probably did. He'd have to be very, very careful or she'd put two and two together and come up with four.

How Whitney would react if and when she learned that he was the town's mystery benefactor was pretty predictable. She'd be fit to be tied.

Or maybe worse.

Whitney thought about Josh and his admittedly barren childhood all the way home. What a shame that he had missed out on so much fun as a boy. There was no way to actually make up for his upbringing, of course, but she intended to give it a try.

Pulling the Mustang into the empty side of the double garage, she used her remote to close the door behind her before getting out of the car. It was a tight fit these days. Ever since her dad's recent knee surgery, her mother had been doing all the driving. Consequently, their SUV was crowded to the right of center, leaving Whitney a lot less room to maneuver in the space that was left for her.

She grabbed her tote and managed to wiggle it out after her, then headed for the house. The moment she opened the kitchen door, the enticing aromas of an Italian meal made her mouth water.

Not seeing anyone at the table or any food left on the stove, she called, "I'm home! I hope you saved me some supper. I'm starving."

"In the refrigerator," her mother answered. "How was the party in the park?"

That was a question Whitney had been asking herself

all the way home. Her so-called investigation was getting nowhere, but her interest in one of the merchants seemed to be making great progress. Whether that was good or bad, however, was yet to be determined.

Shorter than her daughter, with hair a couple of shades darker blond, Betty joined Whitney in the kitchen and started to pull containers of leftovers out of the fridge. "So, tell me what happened tonight."

"The same old, same old," Whitney said, shedding her coat, scarf and gloves before turning back around. The moment she saw her mother's face she knew her excuse had fallen flat.

"Oh, really? Then why are you blushing?"

"My cheeks are just chapped from the frosty air."

Betty chuckled as she dished spaghetti and meat sauce onto a plate and slipped it into the microwave. "Whitney, I have known you for twenty-five years. You were never a good fibber, which is a blessing for any mother. Now, let's have it. What's going on?"

"Well, I did invite Josh Smith to come here for Christmas dinner. His mother is going to be away and he has no other family."

"Good for you. There's nothing wrong with that."

"He turned me down."

Frowning, the older woman studied her daughter. "Did he? That's a bit odd. Isn't he going to be lonesome?"

"He says not." Whitney gave a shrug. "So, I thought maybe, if we asked him to dinner before that, he might relax and change his mind about coming here for Christmas." She sighed as the fresh aromas from her reheating food reached her. "I told him what a great cook you are."

"Thanks. When should I expect him?"

"We didn't settle on a date. I told him we'd probably see him in church tomorrow morning. Is that all right?"

"Fine with me." Betty laughed softly and arched her eyebrows, indicating the other room. "Your father will want to meet your young man, anyway."

"Whoa!" Whitney's hands shot up as if she were being accosted at gunpoint. "Josh is not *my* anything. He's just a lonesome guy with nowhere to go for Christmas. If he does decide to join us it will be as a family friend. Nothing more. Okay?"

Whitney would have felt a lot more reassured if her mother had not given her an exaggerated wink and another soft laugh.

True, it was going to be a bit awkward introducing everyone in public on Sunday but that couldn't be helped. At least she only had one more night to worry about it. Besides, what could go wrong at church? They'd be among friends and her parents were pretty easygoing. Plus, she was no teenager with a crush.

Of course not.

She was a mature woman—with a crush.

"That is so stupid," she muttered to herself. "Get a grip."

Betty handed her the plate of hot food. "What was that, honey?"

"Nothing. Just talking to myself."

"I used to do that all the time, too," Betty said. "It started right after I met your father and didn't stop until...well, I guess it never has stopped entirely." She cast a fond eye in the direction of the living room where J.T. was resting and watching television.

"How's Dad feeling today? I figured his knee must be bothering him when you two didn't show up at the park."

"It's still hard for him to stand for very long. If he wasn't so stubborn about not wanting to use a cane he'd probably have more stamina. Knee replacements are no fun but it's better than not being able to walk at all."

"I'm surprised you two are getting along so well since he's not himself."

Betty laughed. "Honey, your father may have his faults but we still love each other, even after all our years of marriage." Her voice mellowed then caught. "If you ever find a man half as wonderful as your daddy, hang on tight and don't ever let him go."

Although Whitney seemed focused entirely on her plate, she found herself picturing a certain reclusive barista and wondering how she could hang on tight to him when she didn't seem able to get a good grip in the first place.

Chapter Six

Josh almost managed to talk himself into skipping church that Sunday. He didn't know a lot about the Bible yet, but he knew enough to feel guilty if he failed to honor his commitment to worship regularly with the local congregation. Either he was dedicated to his newfound faith or he wasn't. It was that simple.

The complication was Whitney Leigh, of course. If anyone else in Bygones had invited him to share a meal he wouldn't have thought anything of it. As a matter of fact, he'd joined Chase Rollins, Patrick Fogerty and others for lunch at The Everything more than once. The food wasn't the problem. The woman was.

He'd almost made a big mistake with her in the park the night before. What had gotten into him, anyway? Must have been the party atmosphere or something. There was simply no way she could have gotten under his skin so thoroughly that he forgot who and what he was. Even if she did happen to like him at present, she was going to end up furious when she eventually figured out the truth. And she would. There was no doubt in his mind she wouldn't quit probing until she knew everything.

Josh had left his expensive, hand-tailored suits back home in St. Louis. In order to maintain his modest persona in Bygones, he had adopted a much more casual look. His Sunday best was a pair of pressed jeans topped with a suede blazer or, if the weather was especially frigid as it had been at the tree-lighting, a black leather bomber jacket.

Happily, he'd found that his choice of wardrobe fit the area perfectly. So did letting his hair grow a little longer so it touched his collar in back. One thing he didn't do, however, was refrain from shaving daily. The scruffy look might suit some men, but leaving whisker shadow on his chin had never appealed to Josh.

The parking lot at Bygones Community Church was already half-full when he turned the van into it. He would have driven a personal car if he hadn't been trying to perpetuate the image of a struggling shopkeeper.

The more he thought about his well-planned deception, the more it bothered him, particularly since he'd joined this church. It had occurred to him to confide in Pastor Hugh Garman, and he probably would have, if he had not been worried that the elderly man might insist on full, immediate disclosure of the truth.

Groups of people were hurrying from their cars toward the warm sanctuary. Josh joined them. The crew-cut greeter at the front door shook his hand vigorously and handed him a bulletin. "Good morning! Glad you could make it."

Josh returned his wide grin, said, "Yeah, me, too, Don," and meant it from the bottom of his heart. It was that kind of total acceptance that he craved. As CEO and founder of Barton Technologies he was always treated with due respect at the office, yet that was not the same as the sense of belonging he'd found right here. Not even close.

Whitney and a middle-aged couple were waiting in the small vestibule at the rear of the sanctuary. The woman looked like a slightly older version of Whitney. The man, who was obviously her father, was scowling and leaning on a cane with both hands.

Josh approached the family with a smile. "Good morning. You must be Whitney's dad." He offered his hand but the man ignored it.

"That, I am."

Whitney interrupted to make proper introductions. "Josh Smith, meet Betty and J.T., my parents."

"My pleasure," Josh said. He could tell that Betty was okay with everything. J.T., however, was another story.

"We're delighted to meet you, Josh," Betty said, taking his hand and holding it for a brief moment before elbowing her husband and prodding him. "Shake the man's hand, you old coot. Don't forget you're in a house of worship."

For an instant, Josh saw a clear reflection of Whitney in her mother's words and actions. It was obvious she had passed along plenty of mannerisms and inflections as well as the intelligence he'd found so appealing—as long as the cute reporter wasn't using it to pry into his private life, that is.

Josh once again extended his hand. "I guess we'd better get along or the women folk are going to pitch a fit," he said quietly.

The older man nodded, shifted his weight on the cane and shook Josh's hand. "Guess so. I ought to know better than to forget my manners when my wife is around." Although J.T.'s grip was firm, Josh still sensed hesitancy.

"In case you were wondering," Josh offered, "your daughter and I are just friends."

"Good to hear." Demonstrating a change of mood, J.T. clapped him on the shoulder. "We'd better get in there and grab a pew before all the good seats in the back are taken."

"My thoughts exactly," Josh said. "The last thing I want is be stuck in the front row where Pastor Hugh can peer over the top of his glasses and give me one of his knowing stares."

"You got any reason why he'd want to?"

Josh stifled a laugh. "Nope. From what I've seen since I joined this church, he doesn't need a good reason. It seems to me he just throws out the notion of sin and sinners, then scoops up whatever rises to the bait."

"I like this guy," J.T. said, winking at his wife. "It's kinda too bad he and Whitney aren't serious about each other."

A frog caught in Josh's throat and almost made him choke. He'd been worried about the Leigh family not accepting him. It was starting to look as if they'd had the opposite reaction. That wasn't good, either, but he supposed it beat total rejection.

Or did it? Josh helped Whitney shed her coat while both women let J.T. lead the way into one of the pews and position himself to protect his healing knee. That meant that Betty was between her husband and daughter, leaving Josh the last seat on the aisle. Right next to Whitney.

He unbuttoned his tan suede blazer as he sat down and looked around. Muted light shone through the high, stained glass windows, carrying beams of color onto the rows of wooden pews. At the front of the sanctuary stood a rustic cross framed by a shallow, white-painted arch.

Normally, there was little else up front except the pulpit, a microphone and a tasteful flower arrangement, but today Lily had outdone herself. There were potted, red poinsettias grouped at the base of the altar area like a fiery garden. And in the center of the cluster were seven white plants, arranged in the shape of a cross. It was so unusual it was garnering everyone's attention.

Josh was about to point it out to Whitney when the overhead lights dimmed and a single spot shone on the white flowers. The pastor, wearing a business suit rather than being robed like the choir, announced, "This season, as we celebrate Christ's birth, we must also remember why He came to dwell among us. Without His miraculous birth,

His death is of no consequence. And without His death and resurrection, there would be no celebration of His birth."

With that, the choir marched in singing the Hallelujah chorus of Handel's *Messiah,* accompanied by an orchestra on a CD.

The congregation rose without being told to.

Whitney slipped her hand through the crook of Josh's elbow as naturally as if they had stood together to worship a hundred times before.

He laid his free hand over hers and closed his eyes. All this was pretty new to him but one thing was apparent. Something special was happening here. To him.

It had begun when he had gone forward a few months ago. Back then, he'd thought that was all there was to it, yet every time he'd set foot in Bygones Community Church since that day he'd learned something new and amazing—about the gospel and about himself.

The congregation was singing along with the choir now. The music had switched to a hymn that sounded familiar to Josh and everyone was joining in without having to read the words.

Except him. Would he ever reach the point where he was able to fully participate the way others did? To be a part of the service instead of feeling like a bystander?

It was his fondest wish that he would.

It was also a reminder that once he left Bygones and went back to St. Louis he might never find a church that was as friendly and accepting as this one.

Or a partner to worship with who was half as perfect as Whitney Leigh.

Whitney didn't remember much of the sermon she'd just heard, primarily because she'd been unable to stop dwelling on the way she'd felt sitting there next to Josh.

After the closing prayer she glanced at her mother and

father. Betty had put on her coat and was helping J.T. with his without being obvious about it. Their relationship had changed since his knee surgery. At times, it seemed they were more quarrelsome, particularly when her father refused to heed his doctors. Other times, like now, Whitney sensed a glow of abiding love.

She had no doubt that that love had been there all along. It had simply taken the stress of his surgery to bring it to the fore.

"You're looking awfully pleased," Betty remarked to her daughter. "It was a beautiful service, wasn't it?"

"Uh-huh. It's also nice to see you and Dad getting along so well."

The older woman's grin spread, crinkling her face at the corners of her eyes and making them sparkle. "Oh, honey. We've always gotten along well, even when it may not have looked like it to outsiders—or even to you. Your father and I have the kind of marriage where we know what the other is thinking before it's even said."

"And finish each other's sentences. I know. I've heard you do that a million times."

"Right." Betty eyed Josh as he stood back politely to let the women proceed up the aisle ahead of him. "I like your friend. And I suspect you do, too."

"Of course, I do. I like all my friends."

"Uh-huh."

"Don't look at me like that," Whitney warned with an arch of her eyebrows.

Rather than block the crowded aisle she chose to move ahead until they were all outside. Bright sun glistened off the piles of snow that had been cleared from the church parking lot by machine.

She shivered and rubbed her hands together. "Brrr. Too bad the Cozy Cup is closed on Sundays. I could use another cup of hot cocoa about now."

"Why don't we all go back to the house together?" Betty was looking straight at Josh as she spoke. "You, too, of course. Maybe you can give me a few tips on making great coffee."

"Not without bringing my espresso machines," he replied. "Am I invited anyway?"

"Of course you are. No sense making a big deal about it. We're having leftovers. You can't get much more casual than that."

"Sure," Josh said with a nonchalant shrug. "Sounds fine to me."

If Whitney had not been so shocked at the ease with which her mother had handled the situation, she might have commented—and ruined everything.

"Okay. See you in a few," Whitney said. Smiling to herself, she left the other three discussing the best route to take to the Leigh house and hurried to her Mustang. Josh was coming to share a meal! "Thank You, Jesus."

She climbed into the car and slipped the key into the ignition, then paused with her hands on the steering wheel and closed her eyes.

"Help me to understand him," she prayed. "I can't imagine how hard it must have been to grow up in a family where there were no special celebrations or times when they shared joy. No wonder he refuses to open up more."

She could picture him as a forlorn child who had channeled all his interest into computers because he'd had nothing else. Well, that was over. He might not know how to be a part of a loving family like hers but she was going to do her best to teach him, to make him feel so welcome he wouldn't hesitate to fill her in about his past. Then, they'd both benefit.

He'd taken the first steps toward opening his life to agape love when he'd joined the church. Being around her mom and dad was going to be the next one.

And then what? she asked herself.

In the back of her mind, beyond where she was willing to venture, was the lingering notion that she might want Josh Smith to become even more to her. Much more.

The Leigh residence was small compared to many of the others on that outlying block of Granary Road. Painted white with blue shutters, it sat far enough back from the street to give Mrs. Leigh room for summer flowerbeds as well as some lawn. Parallel strips of concrete formed the driveway, in the manner of many older homes, and led to a garage that looked as if it had been expanded from its original size.

Josh parked his van in the street and got out, dallying to give his host and hostess time to enter the house ahead of him.

Before they had triggered the automatic garage door to close after their SUV, he'd noticed that Whitney's yellow convertible was already there. She had been unusually subdued this morning. Almost a different person. And that change disturbed him.

Trying to decide if she truly embraced a new persona when she was away from work, or if she had merely been quiet because she was up to something, he started for the front door.

It was jerked open before he had a chance to knock. The silly grin on Whitney's face was so charming, so unexpected, it made him laugh.

She, too, giggled. "Welcome. I'm so glad you could come."

"I gathered as much. I only hope you don't have too many ulterior motives, lady."

"Me?" Blushing, she pressed her fingertips to her neck and stepped back to give him room to enter. "Not me. I am as innocent as a babe."

"I doubt you were totally innocent even when you were still in your crib, Whitney. There's too much going on in that head of yours. I can almost see the wheels turning and smoke coming out of your ears."

"What? You think I was a menace in preschool?"

"Yes. I imagine you told on anybody who broke the rules, even if they didn't get caught until you'd ratted them out."

"Well!"

Still amused, Josh stepped into the compact living room. J.T. was already ensconced in a brown tweed recliner with his legs elevated. He signaled to Josh to have a seat nearby.

"You're right about Whitney," her father said pleasantly. "I have never known a bigger busybody—in a good way, of course. She has this thing about digging up the whole truth, no matter what."

A shiver shot up Josh's spine. "I'd assumed as much."

"Oh, you don't know the half of it."

"Dad! That's enough. Josh isn't interested in your exaggerated stories about me."

"I might be," he drawled, working hard to seem casual in spite of the clenching of his gut. "But there's no hurry. I'm sure your mom would like to volunteer her opinions, too."

Tossing her head and rolling her eyes, Whitney flounced out of the room, leaving both men grinning broadly.

J.T. shifted his position and grimaced. "Not supposed to sit in one position too long. Those wooden pews absolutely kill me."

"But still you go to church."

"Yeah. Seems like the right thing to do. You know, because the good Lord's blessed me so much." His expression relaxed and mellowed. "I've got a great wife, a fairly easy life compared to lots of men, a smart daughter and a roof over my head. What more could I want?"

"Better knees?" Josh offered.

"They would've been fine if I hadn't played football in college. I blew one back then and it hasn't been right since. Finally had to have the thing replaced." He swept his palm over his thinning hair. "Don't care if I go bald, just don't want to have to be pushed around in a wheelchair if I can help it. I'm bored enough as it is."

"I can understand that." Josh looked around the room. "What do you do for entertainment?"

"Nothing much. I'm sure sick of TV."

"What about surfing the web? Do you have a personal computer?"

"Only a laptop like Whitney uses. She gave me her old one but I never have been able to make it work right."

"I can take a look at for you if you'd like. I'm pretty handy with those things."

"So my daughter tells me. Did you go to school or learn it on your own?"

"A little of both. My mind just seems to grasp the concepts. I don't know why."

"Well, I think it's over there in that cabinet under the TV. I'd appreciate it if you could do something with it. Everybody tells me the same thing. Time would pass faster if I could keep my mind occupied."

"I totally agree." Rising, Josh found the laptop and carried it back to the sofa where he opened it. "First off, charging the batteries would help."

"I don't know where the cord or anything is. Why don't you take it with you when you leave and I'll have Whitney pick it up for me after you're done checking it out. If it's toast, maybe my wife will take pity on me and buy me a new one."

"I might have a spare unit lying around my place that I could loan you," Josh told him just as Whitney and Betty started carrying food from the kitchen into the dining room.

J.T. snorted. "Will you look at that? Eating in the kitchen

is good enough for me but you get the company treatment. I don't know whether to be happy for the extra pampering or offended that they don't do it all the time."

"Hush, you old complainer," Betty said, making a face at him. "You've had personal maid service for weeks. It's time you made an effort to get back to normal."

"See what I have to put up with?" J.T. said to Josh before giving him a sly wink. "Women. They think they run the world."

"If we did, there would probably be less trouble," his wife said. She pointed to a chair on her right. "Josh, you sit here."

"Is there anything I can help you with?" he asked.

"You're our guest this time," Whitney answered for her mother.

"*This* time?" One of Josh's eyebrows arched and he gave her a lopsided smile. "Will there be other times?"

"Maybe. If you mind your manners," Betty teased. "Now, if everybody will please sit down so J.T. can say the blessing, we'll eat. I'm starved."

Josh waited until he had seen where the others were going to sit so he could pull out chairs for both women. It was no surprise when Whitney ended up next to him on one side of the table and her parents occupied the other.

What did come as rather a shock was the poignant prayer her father offered to bless the food. Coming from the plain-speaking, gruff, older man, it reflected a tenderness, a love of God, that was totally unexpected.

So was the ambience that surrounded them. For the first time, Josh was beginning to understand why Whitney kept expressing sympathy for the way he'd been raised. His upbringing had not prepared him for this kind of family life. These people did have something special, something intangible that bound them together.

The sad part was that he was on the outside, looking

in, and probably always would be. It was a comfort to pretend he was a part of their world for an hour or two, but the truth was clear.

He came from a totally different background. He and Whitney were poles apart. And no amount of wishing was ever going to change that fact.

Chapter Seven

If Whitney had not relished the very same meal the night before, she would have wondered what had happened to her mother's culinary expertise. The food was identical, yet she could hardly force down a bite, let alone appreciate it.

Josh was seated politely to her right. As far as Whitney's imagination was concerned, they might as well have been sharing the same chair! Everything about him seemed magnified, from his woodsy aftershave to the broad shoulders beneath the leather of his suede jacket.

His mere presence was overwhelming. She had thought it was strong when they'd sat in church together but that was mild compared to the vibes she was getting now.

Talk. Say something witty, she told herself. Nothing came to mind—except for the intense, unsettling feelings regarding their guest—and she could hardly voice those!

"This is delicious, Mrs. Leigh," Josh said. "Whitney was right. You're a wonder in the kitchen."

"Thank you. But please, call me Betty."

"Okay, Betty." Josh put down his fork and leaned slightly forward as if to share a confidence with his hostess. "Tell me, did Whitney really almost burn the house down trying to cook?"

J.T. snorted. "Which time?"

Whitney could have crawled under the table with embarrassment. “Dad…”

She could tell from her father’s expression that he was not about to hold back when he had such a willing audience.

Striking a thinker’s pose, he drew his fingers and thumb down opposite sides of his jaw. When they met below his chin he nodded. “Let’s see. There was the time she was making hardboiled eggs and got distracted by something on her computer. The next thing we knew there was egg all over the ceiling.” He chortled. “Did you know that after the water is all boiled away those shells will blow up like a bomb? Well, they will. Threw gobs of egg everywhere. I thought somebody was setting off grenades in the kitchen.”

Whitney rested her forehead on her hand, elbow on the table, and moaned. “I’d forgotten all about that one.”

“Guess your folks haven’t,” Josh offered. He grinned across at his host. “Are there more?”

Betty elbowed her husband. “We’ve heard enough.”

“Aw, I was just getting to the best one. Remember the Christmas coffee cake?”

“The one where the fire department was called?” Josh asked. “She told me about that. Did she really set the oven for self-cleaning instead of bake?”

“Yup. Filled the whole place with so much smoke I didn’t think we’d ever get the smell out of the carpets. Betty had to buy new drapes.”

“Which we sorely needed,” the older woman said.

Whitney’s father was laughing softly and grinning, obviously recalling other incidents. She hoped he’d have the good sense to listen to her mother’s advice and keep them to himself.

Surprisingly, Josh came to her rescue. “Maybe you should save some of the funny stories for another time. I think your daughter is fighting the urge to kick you under the table and we wouldn't want her to damage your sore knee."

Did this mean that Josh was willing to revisit them? It sure sounded like it. Whitney caught her mother's attention and arched an eyebrow.

Betty was ready. "Speaking of other times, how about joining us for Christmas dinner, Josh?"

"Well, I…"

"It won't be fancy, if that's what you're worried about. Just the usual. Ham, candied yams, fruit salad, green beans and homemade pumpkin and mince pies."

It took him a moment to answer. When he did, Whitney's spirits soared and she had to stifle the wide grin that kept trying to take over her expression.

"I suppose we could consider it a trade," Josh said. "J.T. gave me a laptop that needs repair. When I have it fixed and bring it back I'd love to share another meal with you. It doesn't have to be on Christmas."

"Of course not," Betty said quickly. "You're welcome here anytime. With or without the computer. And if you're free on Christmas day you can come then, too. We always have plenty."

"Mom could feed half the town," Whitney added. "She makes enough to give us leftovers for a week."

"That's the easy way," Betty said. "Years ago, when I was still working, I started cooking big batches of food that would last us for several days. There's less cleanup that way, too."

"Where did you work?" Josh asked.

"I was an insurance claims investigator," Betty told him. "It was like a game to me. The more cheaters I managed to catch, the better I liked it."

Josh's attention went from one of the women to the other, settling on Whitney as his guilt blossomed. "Like mother, like daughter?"

"Not exactly," Whitney countered. "Mom was chasing crooks. All I've done lately is write about engagements and weddings." She took a deep breath and released it as a sigh. "I sure wish I could get the scoop on Mr. Moneybags and amaze my boss at the *Gazette.* He might even give me a byline."

"Well," Betty mused, "how about asking Josh to help you? He's the computer expert. Maybe he can trace some facts for you."

"Yes! Like the email addresses to the corporation that handled the funding! All my efforts were a dead end."

Josh was shaking his head. He put his fork down with deliberately studied slowness and leaned away from the table. "Hacking is illegal."

"It wouldn't be hacking, per se," Whitney countered. "All I need is for you to check some of the old emails that Coraline received and see if you can pinpoint their origins."

"That sounds like hacking to me."

Whitney shrugged. "Okay. If you won't help me, I suppose I can find somebody else. Maybe one of the teens who frequents your store will be smart enough."

He held up his hands, palms toward her, in surrender. "Okay. You've made your point. I can't let you lead those innocent kids astray. Bring me the information and I'll see what I can do."

Delighted, Whitney high-fived one of his raised hands. "Deal!"

There was no way Josh was going to provide the information Whitney wanted in a timely manner, but he figured it was prudent to keep her from involving others in her quest. He knew full well where those email addresses would lead and whose name would eventually surface. His. At least his real name.

Given the nosy reporter's keen mind, it would not take

her long to figure out that Josh Smith and Josh Barton were one and the same. Surely he could continue to stall her for a few more weeks.

The more he got to know Whitney, the more tempting it was to confide in her, although he knew better. She was dedicated to her job to the point where it posed a real threat to his anonymity. Once she knew everything, there was no way he could expect her to keep his secret. Not when she had been actively seeking his identity for almost six months.

Carrying her father's broken laptop and standing at the Leighs' door, he offered an amiable farewell.

"Thanks for inviting me," he said, looking from Betty to J.T., then focusing on Whitney.

"Like I said, you're welcome anytime," Betty told him. "Good night."

Night? Was it? Had he been there all afternoon and into the evening?

Josh glanced out the half-open door and paused. The sun was setting. "Whoa. It is getting dark. I had no idea I'd stayed so long." He studied Whitney's lovely face. "I hope I haven't kept you from something else you wanted to do."

"There is nothing I would rather do on a Sunday afternoon than relax with family and friends," she said, stepping out onto the porch with him and folding her arms when the cold hit her. "Besides, you helped wash dishes. I'll take that kind of offer any day."

"Guess I'm used to it from the coffee shop," Josh said. *But never has it been so enjoyable.* The time he and Whitney had spent cleaning up the kitchen together had been fun. Their conversations had been personal without being intrusive. And they had found so many opportunities to laugh he was still basking in the pleasing aftereffects.

"Thanks, anyway. It was sweet of you to pitch in."

"You're quite welcome." He lifted the laptop as he added,

"I'll see what I can do with this ASAP. I think it would do your dad a lot of good to be able to connect to the internet and stimulate his mind. It's not good to sit and brood."

"I totally agree. That's one reason I gave it to him in the first place. I suspect the problem is more the operator than the device."

Josh saw her shiver. "You'd better get back inside before you catch cold." He took a step away. "See you."

"Absolutely." She gave him a conspiratorial grin. "We have a mystery to solve. I feel so much better knowing you'll be helping me."

If Josh had felt any more culpable he'd have kicked himself. The openness and trust Whitney was demonstrating were enough to make him want to confess then and there.

He wouldn't, of course. He was a planner, not someone who acted on a whim. There was a right and a wrong way to go about revealing his identity if he chose to do so. Shivering in the snow while standing on a tiny front porch was neither the time nor the place.

It had occurred to him, more than once, to give Whitney the scoop she'd been seeking. The better he got to know her, the more tempting it was, particularly since he was starting to care what she thought of him, personally.

The only way he would feel comfortable allowing himself to get much closer to her was if they were presenting their real selves. She was doing so, of course. But he was still hiding behind a false identity.

When he had originally decided to come to Bygones undercover, he had not anticipated wanting to drop the guise of a struggling merchant until the project had reached its six-month anniversary. Now, he was becoming sorely conflicted.

For the first time since he had originally come up with the concept of rescuing the main street in tiny Bygones, Kansas, he was seriously questioning his devious approach.

If he had been a Christian at the outset, would he have misrepresented himself? He doubted it. But now that he was in this deep, how in the world was he going to extricate himself without causing undue pain and disappointment?

Josh had absolutely no idea.

The moment Whitney stepped back into the house and closed the front door, her mother cheered.

"Wahoo! Good for you, honey. Well done."

Making a silly face, Whitney shook her head. "I don't know. I like Josh and all. It's just that there's something off about him. Know what I mean?"

"Don't be silly," Betty insisted. "He's just shy. Didn't you notice how he started to relax as the afternoon went on?"

From his recliner, J.T. hooted. "Should have seen your face when I was telling him about those exploding eggs."

"That was not your finest hour, Dad."

"Nonsense. Can't act formal and expect a guy to loosen up. When I was dating your mother I was scared to death of her father. I don't think he ever smiled at me until he walked her down the aisle at our wedding."

Whitney blanched. "Whoa. Let's have no wedding talk. Don't either of you start playing matchmaker. I am not planning to fall into the same trap so many of the newbies have lately. Looking at those statistics, a person would think there were no eligible singles in Bygones before they arrived."

"I wouldn't go quite that far," Betty countered. "But I do think those new business folks are the cream of the crop. After all, the SOS committee did vet them all."

"True." Whitney plopped into one of the side chairs next to the fireplace. "They seem to have been meant for Bygones. All except one. I can't explain why. I just think Josh Smith is different, somehow."

"Maybe that's because you like him too much," her

mother suggested. When Whitney opened her mouth to reply, Betty held up a hand like a traffic cop. "Don't deny it. I don't know if Josh can tell how you feel, but I sure can. When you look at him your eyes get all misty. You blush too much, too. I don't think I've ever seen you react that way, not even when your hunky date picked you up for your senior prom."

"Don't be ridiculous. I'm not a flighty teenager anymore. I don't get schoolgirl crushes."

But you do, Whitney admitted to herself as she bid her parents good-night, grabbed her tote and escaped to her room. This was not the first time such a phenomenon had occurred to her, it was simply the first time someone else had accused her of being romantically interested in Josh.

Was she? Until the man stopped being so mysterious and filled her in about his past, she would be a fool to let herself even consider falling for him.

Opening her laptop computer and plugging it in so she wouldn't run down the battery, she seated herself at her desk and waited while it booted up.

One of the first things she intended to do was check the rosters of community colleges in the Midwest. Even if Josh didn't finish a four-year education he might have taken classes at a JC. Of course, nothing said he had to have done so nearby. He could have gotten his training anywhere, even in Alaska or Hawaii, although she thought she'd detected some colloquialisms in his speech that pointed to a more Midwest upbringing.

Encouraging herself, Whitney began by checking social media sites for Josh Smiths.

When the initial search engine listed thousands and thousands of possibilities she stared, sat back and sighed. Finding the proverbial needle in a haystack would be easier than pinning down a guy named Smith.

There had to be another way.

The cord to her computer caught her eye. Gave her an idea. Made her pulse jump. Was it silly to venture out at night or would she be losing a golden opportunity if she discounted a perfectly good idea?

Before she could talk herself out of it she jerked open the bottom drawer of her desk, pawed through the odds and ends in it, and came up with what she needed.

It was the ideal excuse. Josh lived and worked in the same building. She was going to deliver the power cord for the old laptop to him. And she was going to do it now, tonight, when there would be no distractions from his shop customers and they could converse casually.

"Let him come up with a valid excuse to avoid my questions then," Whitney muttered, discounting the notion that her plan was terribly contrived and transparent. "Just let him try."

Chapter Eight

Josh was hopeful as he carried the laptop into his workroom in the rear of the Cozy Cup Café. Whitney said she had deleted her work files before she'd passed her old computer to J.T. but that didn't matter to a pro like Josh. Short of melting the motherboard with a blowtorch or running over it with an army tank, there was no way to wipe old files so well that a person with his expertise could not restore them. Since the laptop had been literally handed to him, his only real problem was one of personal ethics.

First chance he got, he'd ask permission to access Whitney's research files so he could see how far her investigation had gone before she'd upgraded to the new laptop. In the meantime, he'd satisfy himself by checking public areas, like her anti-virus software and malware. Computer forensics was like a fascinating puzzle calling to him to be solved.

He noted that Whitney had carefully backed up her systems. She was thorough. And tenacious. Therefore, he would be wise to start avoiding her as much as possible. If he had not promised to help her with computer searches and to repair this laptop for her father, keeping his distance would have been a *lot* easier.

Evasion from now on was imperative, he realized with

chagrin. The more time he spent in her company, the worse he felt about deceiving her. Distancing himself was not going to be easy, but it was definitely necessary.

A loud rapping on the door of the closed coffee shop startled him. Everybody knew there were no Main Street stores open on Sundays, let alone this late, so who could be knocking?

Josh peered out through the curtain separating the back room from the shop. There was someone at the door, all right. And judging by the greenish blue scarf and gloves his visitor was wearing, he knew who it was.

Assuming she hadn't spied him through the frosty glass, he started to let the curtain fall back into place. It was too late. Whitney began waving her arms and gesturing wildly.

As he reluctantly started for the front door he realized what she was holding. She'd located the charging cable for the old laptop and was apparently intent on delivering it.

He took a deep breath and released it as a sigh while he unlocked the door. "You didn't have to bother to bring that. I told your dad I have extras. I've already got his unit booted up."

Instead of backing off and going home as he'd hoped, Whitney grinned and forged past him into the dimly lit café. "Super. He'll be glad to hear it. What all was wrong with it?"

"Nothing that I could see offhand," Josh replied, slow to follow her yet not wanting to be inhospitable, particularly since her family had just opened their home to him.

"It isn't ready yet," he warned. "I'm good, but I'm not *that* good."

"I wasn't expecting instant results." She gave a light laugh and removed her glasses. "Oops. I'm fogging up."

"So, I see. Why did you come out in the cold in the first place?"

"I guess because I felt bad about my father's asking you

to look at the computer. It worked fine when I gave it to him and he's barely used it. I suspect you're wasting your time tinkering with it. There's probably not a thing wrong that Dad's taking a tutorial wouldn't fix."

"Maybe so. It worked fine as soon as I plugged it in to run the updates." He eyed the chord she was still holding in her gloved hands. "I really won't need that. Why don't you take it home and put it where it won't get misplaced again?"

"Are you trying to get rid of me, Mr. Smith?"

"Of course not. It's just late. I don't want anybody driving past to see us in here and think I've opened on the Sabbath."

"Perish the thought." Whitney cleared her throat, making Josh wonder if she was as nervous as he was.

"We also don't want to start rumors," he offered. "You know how fast gossip travels in a small town."

"Faster than greased lightning, as Miss Ann Mars always says. Don't you just love her? I hope I'm half as agile and quick-witted as she is when I'm in my eighties."

If you get any smarter, I'm a goner, he thought, letting his ensuing words reflect the admiration he felt. "If your current intellect is any sign, I'm sure you'll be just as sharp."

"Why, thank you!"

Pink color flooded her cheeks and he noticed that her green eyes were sparkling in spite of the dim lighting in the front area of his shop. The least he could do, he supposed, was offer her something hot to drink before she started home.

"Can I fix you a mocha latte? You liked that before."

"You remembered. I'm flattered. Are you sure it's not too much trouble?"

"No. It's easy. When I'm here alone I often raid the coffee machines. Couldn't see brewing a regular pot upstairs when I had all this specialty stuff down here."

"That's right. I heard you lived upstairs." She had stepped back to give him better access to the supplies behind the counter. Now, she circled and approached the curtain that separated off his workroom. "So, what's back here?"

Josh's first reaction was to stop her. Then he remembered that not only was she a novice around computers, he had all his real work up in his apartment. There would be nothing for Whitney to see that would jeopardize his continuing charade.

"Work benches and spare parts, mostly. And bulk supplies for the coffee part of the shop. Not very interesting, I'm afraid."

"Okay. Sorry to be so nosy. I guess it's just part of who I am."

"Who are you, exactly?" Josh asked.

Whitney scowled at him. "What do you mean?"

"What are your goals, your aspirations? You're usually so busy asking everybody else leading questions I just wondered what makes you tick."

She chuckled again, seeming ill-at-ease. "Speaking of ticking, Dad says I'm like a two-dollar watch that's been wound too tight. I guess that saying's a holdover from the days when people had to wind their watches instead of relying on batteries."

Although he was measuring freshly ground beans into the espresso machine, Josh managed to arch an eyebrow in her direction. "And you accuse me of not answering questions?"

"Okay, okay." Whitney took off her gloves and stuffed them into her coat pockets before waving her hands. "You win. I was always interested in creative writing. My senior year I was editor of the school paper and co-advisor of the yearbook committee."

"How about college?"

"I took a few journalism classes at the JC up in Manhattan. But I felt as if I was wasting my time studying abstracts when I could be actually working for Ed Kowalski at the *Gazette*." She spread her arms wide. "So, here I am."

"How did you get your newspaper job in the first place?" He was adding foamy milk to the coffee as he spoke.

"Persistence." She laughed lightly, sounding less apprehensive this time. "I must have written over a dozen pieces before Ed accepted one of them. Since I know practically everybody in town, it's easy for me to get interviews and come up with lots of human interest stories and he knows it, so I was a natural."

"Is that what you're doing regarding the Save Our Streets project?" He presented the hot drink with a flourish.

"In a manner of speaking." Whitney accepted the mug and wrapped both hands around it. "Thanks. You know I did a series of columns about the romance angle. But there's a bigger scoop behind everything. I just know it. All I have to do is keep digging." She took a cautious sip. "Mmm. Delicious. Which is where you come in, Mr. Smith."

"Me?" Josh was beginning to feel like a specimen stuck to a slide under the lens of a microscope. "What can I do?"

"Just what you promised," she reminded him. "I have high hopes that tracing that obscure email address will provide the lead I need."

"And if it doesn't?"

"Then we'll try something else."

"We, *kemosabe?*" As he had hoped, his gibe made Whitney chuckle. Her voice was always pleasing to his ears and when she laughed there was something about the sound that lifted his spirits immeasurably.

"Yes, we. I have witnesses that you promised to help me, remember?"

"I don't think it's fair to involve your parents."

"Sorry. Too late." She made more sounds of contentment as she continued to carefully sip the rich drink. "This is wonderful. Maybe even better than the last special one you made me."

"It's exactly the same," Josh insisted.

"In that case," Whitney countered, lowering her lashes and concentrating on the steaming mug, "it must taste better because we spent the day together."

"That makes absolutely no sense."

"Has it ever occurred to you that there are some things that simply *are*—whether you can come up with a plausible reason for them or not?"

"Like what?"

"Like faith," Whitney said, sobering. "It may not make a lot of sense to believe in God, yet you and I do."

He had to admit she had a point. "All right. Granted, our faith may be a stretch for some people. I tried to analyze why I chose to believe when I had my first glimmer of spiritual understanding, but I never came up with a suitable explanation."

"That's because faith can't be reasoned. It either is, or it isn't. I guess you could say it's more of a choice. Now that I've made it, I'd never want to go back."

Josh nodded. "Neither would I. There are times when it seems as if I've always been a Christian. Other times I feel like a total dunce."

"Speaking of dunces," Whitney drawled, "what should I tell Dad about the laptop? I'm almost as big a novice around computers as he is."

"Tell him I want to run more diagnostics on it before I bring it back to him. And I'll need his password if I'm going to double-check his email account."

"There's a file in the laptop that has all our passwords in it. Just help yourself to whatever you want to look at. We have no deep, dark secrets."

"Don't you think keeping them in a file like that is dangerous?"

"Not at all," Whitney said. "There's nothing on there that needs to be kept private. Besides, any hacker worth his salt could probably access anything he wanted, whether he had my passwords or not."

"Not ethically or legally."

"Well, you now have my express permission," Whitney said, draining her drink and shivering slightly. "So you're covered. Have at it. Knock yourself out."

"You're sure?"

"Positive." Setting aside the empty mug she started to put her gloves back on. "Thanks for the warm-up. I know it was silly to come out tonight just to bring you the power cord. I acted on a whim." She glanced through the window at the snowy street. "Now that I'm here and warm again, I hate to go back out there."

"Really, I..."

"Oh, don't panic," Whitney said with a smirk. "I didn't mean I was actually staying."

"I never thought you did."

"Right. And that's why you look so relieved all of a sudden." She started toward the door. "I'll be back tomorrow or the next day with the email addresses I want you to trace."

Josh considered trying to talk her out of it, then remembered what she'd said about recruiting one of his teenage customers. There were a couple of them, including Matt Garman, who might be savvy enough to get her the answers she sought. The way Josh saw the situation, the only way to avoid that was to take on the job himself and see that there were no usable results until after Christmas.

"All right," he said as he unlocked the door to let her out. "Make it in the afternoon. That's our slowest time."

When she turned her emerald gaze on him and smiled, he wondered if she had any idea what mayhem she was causing in his mind and body. The touch of her gloved hand on his forearm was enough to make him tremble.

Instead of leaving immediately, she stood very still, very close to him, and seemed to be waiting. Her eyes misted. Her cheeks warmed. Her lips parted ever so slightly.

It was all Josh could do to keep from bending closer and kissing her. Did she know? Was she taunting him? Or was she as oblivious to her own charms as she seemed?

"Thank you. For everything," Whitney finally said, effectively breaking the mood. "You'd better go make yourself a hot drink. You're shivering."

As Josh closed the door and watched her cautiously pick her way through the snow to her car, he realized that she was right. He was literally quaking in his boots. And it had a lot less to do with the weather than it did with a certain lovely reporter with a tenacious nose for news.

He returned Whitney's farewell wave and watched her climb into her car.

What he wanted to do was run to the curb and… *And what?* he asked himself. The choices his mind provided ranged from hugs to kisses to escorting her home, none of which were the least bit acceptable.

That very evening he had vowed to avoid the woman, yet here he stood, fantasizing about stealing a kiss and coming within a heartbeat of doing so!

Was he crazy? Probably.

Was he a fool? Undoubtedly.

Was he going to be able to follow his own advice and stay away from Whitney Leigh? No way.

The drive home gave Whitney plenty of time to think. Her creative imagination had been running wild tonight, particularly where the handsome barista was concerned. One complimentary cup of coffee had her visualizing being in his arms and accepting his tender kiss.

Whitney huffed. "Accepting, nothing. You wanted to kiss him back and you know it, only he never gave you the chance," she mumbled, disgusted with herself and wondering when she had become such a pushover?

She had always been kind of drawn to Josh. That was a given. But when had simple attraction morphed into the desire to be held in his arms? To be romanced? She was beyond that kind of silliness, wasn't she? She'd certainly thought so until recently.

Some of the townspeople whom she had interviewed had hinted at love at first sight. That was not the case regarding Josh Smith. Whitney had slowly grown to like him. A lot. And the change had taken place so smoothly she could not put her finger on a specific date or event when it had occurred.

They had interacted before, of course. Josh had helped in the community garden as well as providing a venue for a mini-celebration after Gracie's cancelled wedding. And he had joined her and others when they had volunteered to fix up homes in Bygones that needed refurbishing. But that was camaraderie, not romance.

Whitney supposed she might have been influenced by her mother's suggestions regarding Josh, although Betty had tried matchmaking before to no avail. Come to think of it, so had Miss Coraline. What was different this time?

The man, she admitted with chagrin. The man was different. He was Josh, and he was the most interesting, appealing character she had met in who knows when.

So, what was she going to do? she wondered absently.

The answer was so plain when it came, she imagined she might have heard an actual voice saying, "Nothing."

Of all the conclusions she might have drawn, that was the least acceptable. And the most sensible, of course.

Whitney shook her head and sighed. Would God have

led her to get to know Josh if He had not wanted her to fall for him?

Who knew? Certainly not Whitney. One of her biggest problems had always been a lack of sufficient patience. This instance was no different.

In the case of Josh Smith, however, she had no choice but to bide her time.

However, that did not mean she had to *like* it.

Chapter Nine

Gray-haired Coraline Connolly was among those waiting at the door when Josh opened his shop the following morning. He greeted her warmly, then went about the business of serving customers at the counter.

As soon as Josh was able, he poured Coraline's usual cup of Kona, grabbed a cream pitcher and joined her. She had chosen the most private of the small, glass-topped tables and made herself comfortable.

"Here you go, Miz Coraline," he said amiably. "What brings you here so early?"

"I wanted to talk to you before school started," she said, smiling. "How's business?"

"Very good, thanks. The SOS committee should be delighted."

"We are."

Josh watched her smile wane and saw concern in her steady glance. "Then what's bothering you? You look as if you just lost your best friend."

"Not the best, necessarily, but I have suffered a sort of loss."

He reached across the narrow space and patted her hand. "Is there anything I can do?"

"Beyond all you've already done, you mean?"

Scowling, he regarded her. "Beg your pardon?"

"It was that quirky smile of yours that finally clinched it for me, you know. I knew you reminded me of someone but I just couldn't seem to put my finger on who. Then, at the park, I saw you smiling and it all came together." Her expression was kind, her tone soothing. "How is your mother, dear?"

"What? I don't understand." Josh could not have been more surprised if the school principal had started dancing on the table top.

"Susanna. I knew her as Susanna Hastings, of course. She went away to college and never came back to live in Bygones after her parents were killed in that terrible accident. She married soon after that and had a son. Only her last name is Barton—not Smith."

His shoulders slumped. He clasped his hands together on the table and stared. "You know? How much?"

"Enough," Coraline said. "What puzzles me is the masquerade. Why do that? Did you think we wouldn't take your money if we knew who you were? As near as I can tell, it was earned honestly. That's true, isn't it?"

"Of course." Lowering his voice he leaned closer. "Who else knows? Who have you told?"

"Nobody. Not even your mother. I take it you've kept her in the dark, too, or she surely would have contacted me by now."

"You're right. I want it to be a surprise when I tell her I've stepped in and saved her old hometown just for her. You should have seen how happy she was when she thought there was going to be a reunion, and how hard she took it when you called to cancel for lack of funds."

"That's what brought all this on?"

"Yes. At least that's how I got the original idea. After that, the project kind of morphed into what you see today."

"Amazing." Coraline's brow knit. "But why the charade?

You could have told us who you were and what you wanted to do without all the cloak-and-dagger stuff."

"Could I? Are you sure nobody would have spilled the beans and spoiled my surprise? Mom has a lot of old friends in Bygones. That's why I chose to come here incognito in the first place."

"And why you still haven't told anybody who you are?"

"Yes and no. Part of the choice to keep pretending to be Josh Smith is selfish. I feel accepted here and I'm afraid that once I confess what I'm up to, people will treat me differently." Her look of disbelief prodded him to go on. "Trust me, Miss Coraline. It's happened before."

"So, what did you tell Susanna? I mean, she must have asked where you were and what you were doing."

"She did. Mom thinks I'm away because I've been setting up a new branch of Barton Technologies."

"Are you?" Coraline grew pensive before starting to smile. "That's not a bad, idea, you know. I can think of the perfect property, too. The old Randall Manufacturing plant."

"It was just a ploy so Mom wouldn't worry and I could truly surprise her. I'm not looking to expand."

"Why not? You know we have a good base of talent here. Think of the boon a thriving business like yours would be to Bygones!"

Josh had to agree she had a valid point. This wouldn't be a bad place to open a new facility. "You mentioned Randall. What can you tell me about him? The few times I've met him he seemed pretty down. I asked what happened to make his business fail but he never actually explained."

"Besides the downturn in the economy, you mean? The poor man was jilted. Dumped and divorced. After that he sort of quit trying," Coraline said with a telling sigh. "His wife was not only cruel, she was emotionally blind."

"I take it you knew her?"

"Yes. I knew them both. Robert Randall is one of the nicest, sweetest gentlemen I've ever met. If he hadn't lost hope and incentive, thanks to Linda, that nasty ex of his, his plant would probably have survived a temporary slump. But then we wouldn't be having this conversation, would we?"

"The loss of that one plant almost killed the whole town?"

"That, it did. Randall Manufacturing was our only big employer. When Robert gave up and shut everything down for good, it was like driving the last nail into Bygones's coffin." She began to smile. "And then you came along."

"I told you. I did it for my mother's sake," Josh reiterated. "She always had nothing but nice things to say about this place. I think she'd have moved back here long ago if my father hadn't convinced her a person could never truly recapture what was lost."

"Well, I can't believe the changes your plan has made around here in only six months."

"I agree. Profits are good and getting better all the time."

"So, when are you planning to come clean?"

"I wasn't. Anybody who knows me as Josh Smith would be very disappointed if they learned who I really am." He frowned. "Especially a certain eager-beaver newspaper reporter I could mention."

"It's still the right thing to do," the older woman insisted. "Since you can't go back and tell the whole truth in the first place, which would be my first choice, I think the next best thing is to confess everything as soon as possible."

He shook his head. "I need to wait a bit longer. Whitney's writing a promo for a free movie screening in the refurbished theater for between Christmas and New Year's and I want to get that out of the way first."

"That's all well and good, but what about Whitney's newspaper career? Aren't you going to give her a scoop for the *Gazette* so she can wow her boss?"

Josh's brow furrowed. "It's a little more complicated than that. I'd have to make sure she didn't go ballistic and reveal my secret. I wouldn't blame her for trying to get even with me for stringing her along."

"Sounds to me as if you don't want to damage your relationship. I'd suspected as much when I saw you two together at the tree lighting. Every time you looked at each other the sparks flew."

"It's not that. We're just good friends."

Coraline's eyes crinkled at the corners as her grin spread. "Mister *Smith,* I have worked with children and adults of all ages for my entire professional life. I know people. You can deny it all you want. That won't change what I saw. That girl is crazy about you, and as far as I can tell, you return those feelings. Otherwise, why not just tell her who you are and get it over with?"

"Believe me, it's not that simple. Any friendship we may share right now will be sorely tested when Whitney finds out who and what I am."

"Is there some deep, dark secret about computer geniuses that I haven't heard?"

"No." Josh's expression reflected disgust. "But I can't tell you how many women have thrown themselves at me after they found out I was loaded. Or how many people have crawled out of the woodwork to present plans to spend my money for me. Believe me, it's hard to tell who your real friends are when that happens."

"So you chose to come to Bygones as Josh Smith, barista and amateur computer tech."

"Exactly. And so far it's worked out even better than I had hoped."

"All right." Finishing her coffee, Coraline pushed the cup away and rose. "I'll keep your secret. Temporarily. But I'm warning you, the longer you put off telling Whitney the truth, the harder she's going to take it."

"I'm afraid it's way too late to avoid making her mad. When she does finally realize I'm the mystery money man she's been looking for since summer, she's going to be absolutely furious."

"Probably," Coraline agreed. "But the more she cares for you, the worse it's going to be. It's one thing to be tricked by a stranger and quite another to be played for a fool by someone you trusted." She pulled a face. "If you don't think so, just ask Robert Randall. That poor man has really been through the wringer."

"You sound like more than a casual observer."

"I just hate to see a nice person treated badly, that's all. The same goes for Whitney. I know your motives are pure but that doesn't make it right to continue to pretend. Not where she's concerned."

"I'll think about it," Josh promised. "My mother always did say you were very persuasive."

"Only when I'm sure I'm right," the older woman said. "What are you doing for Christmas, going home to see Susanna?"

"Not this year. She's away on a cruise."

"Would you like to join my family? My three grown kids will be home." She blushed. "And Robert has promised to stop by."

"Actually, I've already been invited to the Leighs," Josh told her.

Coraline beamed. "Excellent. You go. And the first chance you get, have a serious talk with that girl. She deserves the truth and you know it."

Although it pained him to admit it, Coraline was right. He glanced at the calendar on the wall behind the cash register. Another ten days until Christmas Eve, then three more before his theater presentation. He could wait that long.

Besides, Josh mused with a sigh, he had no idea how to broach the subject of his personal wealth with a down-to-earth person like Whitney. If he wasn't careful he might inadvertently scare her away.

That was the *last* thing he wanted to do.

Whitney made sure she had all her ducks in a row before she popped in to see Josh later in the week. Matt was on duty behind the counter.

"Hi. Where's the boss?" she asked enthusiastically.

"In the back, working on computers, of course," the sixteen-year-old answered, cocking his head toward the curtained doorway.

"Think he'll mind if I stick my nose in?"

"Naw. He's cool about that. Just don't ever trespass upstairs. He nearly bit my head off when I made the mistake of looking in his apartment when I needed to find him."

"I'll remember that." She started for the workroom. "Thanks, Matt."

Pulling back the curtain with one hand she saw Josh. He was seated on a tall stool and concentrating on a laptop. Was that hers? Perhaps. It certainly wasn't the only one visible.

"Wow," Whitney said, entering, "This room reminds me of Miss Mars's This 'N' That shop."

"Hey, it's not *that* crammed with stuff," Josh countered, greeting her with a grin. "What brings you here today?"

"I would have stopped in sooner if Ed hadn't sent me to Manhattan drumming up advertising customers."

"You do that, too?"

"I do it all," Whitney said, arching a brow. "I deliver papers to drop spots, load racks and collect money from them, sell ads and, hopefully, write wonderful articles. Since we're only a weekly, there isn't a big demand for my reporting expertise but I keep hoping for my so-called big break."

"I've read your work," Josh said. "You're good."

"Thanks. Maybe someday I'll hit the big-time."

"Is that your goal? To get famous and move away, I mean?"

Whitney shrugged. "I used to think so. Now, I kind of wish I could make a name for myself right here in Bygones. I've been toying with the idea of writing a small town feature that could be syndicated, but I'd need to be pretty well known already to pull that off."

"If anyone can do it, you can," Josh said.

"Thanks." Beginning to feel her cheeks heating up she changed the subject by pointing at his workbench. "Is that Dad's laptop?"

"Yes. All ready to go. I installed a couple of new programs I think he'll like, too."

Curiosity drew her closer until she was almost leaning on Josh's shoulder. "Really? Show me."

As his fingers flew over the keys, Whitney was astonished at the images appearing on the screen. "Wow. That operating speed is impressive. Are you sure this is just a hobby?"

"I manage to do okay," he replied, demonstrating other features. "See this little icon in the top left corner? It's visible whenever the unit is turned on, no matter what program may be running. All J.T. will have to do is click on it and his entire system will check and reboot itself. When it's done, there won't be any glitches left, no matter what mistakes he may have made."

"You mean like those services advertised on TV?"

"Much better. This is all self-contained and it won't cost him a penny."

Astounded, she realized she was gaping. "Really? Suppose he's been surfing and picked up a bug?"

"No sweat. There's a regular virus protection program running all the time. This new feature will provide coverage way beyond that. If he was writing a column like you do, for instance, and this computer went up in smoke, all he'd have to do is remove the special memory card, insert it into another machine, type in his personal code, and all his data would immediately transfer."

"Including the operating systems?"

"Yup. Everything is coded to him, not the laptop. It's also updated every few minutes, depending on the settings."

"Wow." She blinked rapidly and stared at the screen. "That's amazing. Can I put the same program on my new laptop?"

It was Josh's hesitancy that caused her to scowl at him. Surely he didn't think she was asking him for a gift that might be expensive. Or did he?

"I don't mean you have to just give it to me," Whitney assured him. "Or to Dad, either. I'll be glad to buy the special chip or whatever it is." She paused, then added, "Providing it doesn't take my whole salary."

"It's experimental right now," Josh said quietly. "I happen to know a guy who's letting a few folks beta test it. There won't be any charge."

"Really? You just happen to know him? Sounds interesting. What's his name?"

The fact that Josh didn't immediately answer struck her as strange. And troublesome. Short of patience, she prodded him. "Well? If you won't tell me his name, at least give me the name of the program so I can watch for its release."

"I don't think it has a name yet."

"Okay..." Whitney drawled "...then where does he work? I'd love to have the scoop on something this revolutionary. It might mean a chance to be picked up by the national wire services and get my byline really noticed."

"When it's ready, we'll make an official announcement," Josh said flatly. "You have to promise me you won't tell a soul until my friend is ready to go public."

She drew her index finger in an X over her chest. "Cross my heart. Your secret is safe with me."

Josh swiveled the stool to face her and took both her hands in his. "I mean it, Whitney. Not a peep."

His seriousness took her aback. Of all the times they had been together, she could not recall one in which he had looked this somber, not even when she'd almost toppled off a stepladder while painting a house with a group of community volunteers and he had come to her aid.

"I promise." The warmth of his touch seeped into her bones and eliminated any hesitation she might have had. When Josh was holding her hands and looking at her that way, she knew she would have promised him anything he asked.

To her surprise, instead of releasing her, he bent and brushed a kiss across her knuckles. The moment was tender and special, yet Whitney found herself reverting to her usual reaction to any overly serious moment and wanting to crack a joke. That was simply the way her mind worked whenever her emotions became overburdened.

She was smiling when Josh's gaze met hers.

One corner of his mouth quirked in a lopsided grin. "What are you thinking?"

"You don't really want to know," she hedged, hoping he would not press for the truth.

"Ah, but I do." Josh continued to hold her hands while his thumbs stroked them gently.

"Well…" If they had not been alone in the workroom and if she had not been so uptight, she might have chosen to hold back.

Josh's brows arched in unspoken query.

"I can't help it. Honest. I always picture silly things when I get nervous."

"I make you nervous?"

"Oh, yes."

"Well, well."

His quiet chuckle sent tingles shooting up her spine and made the hair at her nape prickle. And still he didn't release her. In fact, he kissed her hands again.

That was all she could take. She huffed, then voiced her secret thoughts. "You missed."

"Beg pardon?"

"You wanted to know what I was thinking before. Well, that was it. You missed."

He slowly stood, bringing them closer together. One hand continued to grasp hers while the other rose. He tipped back her head with one finger under her chin.

Whitney froze, eyes closed and lips slightly parted. He knew exactly what she'd meant.

Time slowed. The surroundings faded. She held her breath. Felt the light touch of Josh's mouth on hers.

And then he was gone.

When Whitney's eyes fluttered open he had stepped away and shoved his hands into the pockets of his jeans.

Before she could say a word or even catch her breath, Josh broke her heart by saying, "Sorry. That won't happen again."

Chapter Ten

The amazingly tender kiss and its disappointing aftermath kept replaying in Whitney's mind so vividly she could hardly think straight, let alone write creatively. She didn't remember leaving the Cozy Cup or driving away with J.T.'s computer, yet she had.

If the weather had been warmer she would have put down the top of her faithful convertible and cruised some country roads to unwind and try to make sense of her feelings. Since that method of release was foolish at this time of year, she chose to drop in on Coraline again.

If the principal was too busy to chat she wouldn't stay, of course. She simply needed someone to listen while she talked her way back to some semblance of good judgment. Her choices of confessor were either Coraline or Pastor Garman. Given the difference in a female point of view, it was easy for Whitney to decide who might understand her better. No way was she going to talk to her mother and trigger Betty's matchmaking efforts again. Opening up to Coraline was risky enough.

Whitney found the older woman in her school office and rapped on the open door.

"Come in, come in. I was just thinking about you," the graying principal said.

"I hope that's good." Whitney had dropped her tote on the floor and plopped into a chair.

"Always, dear. Goodness, did you come out without your gloves? Your hands look frozen."

"They're in my pocket," Whitney told her. "Guess I forgot to put them on." She blew a breath. "It's a long story."

"I have a break coming. Would you like to go to the teacher's lounge for a cup of coffee to warm you up?"

"I may never look at another cup of coffee as long as I live. Do you mind if we stay here?"

"Of course not." Rising, Coraline came out from behind the desk, closed her office door, then returned to the chair beside Whitney. "Go ahead. What's bothering you?"

"Everything."

"Sounds ominous. Let me guess. Josh Smith."

"How did you know?"

"I'm a student of people," Coraline said. "I saw how you and he behaved toward each other at the tree lighting. It doesn't take a genius to figure out your romance is not going the way you want it to."

"I don't know *what* I want," Whitney confessed. "One minute I think we're getting along fine and the next he's backing off as if he isn't at all interested in me."

Coraline patted the back of Whitney's hand. "Believe me, dear, he's interested."

"I thought so, too, when he…"

"What? Did he tell you something special?"

"No." She frowned, remembering. "He kissed me."

"Well, that's a good sign."

Whitney shook her head. "Not when he said it would never happen again!"

"What did you say then?"

"I don't recall. Probably nothing." She pointed. "I just grabbed Dad's refurbished laptop and split."

Pensive, the older woman nodded. "I see."

"Well, I sure don't," Whitney complained. "Josh is a genius with computers yet he's satisfied to tinker with a few of them here and there and run a coffee shop. It makes no sense."

"Have you told him how you feel? I mean personally, not about his career choices?"

"I almost did—until he got mad at himself for kissing me."

"Maybe you left him too soon," Coraline suggested. "Sometimes, when a man seems reluctant, it's because he isn't sure of your feelings and doesn't want to risk rejection." She paused, smiled, then added, "That was what happened between me and Robert, but I finally got him to admit he was willing to start over—with me."

"Robert Randall?" Whitney couldn't help being pleased. "Good for you, Miss Coraline. I wish you two the best."

"Thank you. And the same to you and Josh."

"There is no *me and Josh,*" Whitney countered. "I wish there were. I really do."

"I suspect you're telling that to the wrong person. Why not tell Josh?"

"For the same reason you said Robert held back, I guess. I'd rather hang on to the idea that he might care for me a little than ask him and find out it was all a figment of my imagination."

"He did kiss you."

Whitney heaved a noisy sigh and nodded. "That part was real." She paused, thinking. "I don't want to scare him off by being too bold. He seemed to have a good time when he came to my house for supper after church last Sunday. Maybe it would be best if I just kept inviting him and let everything come together naturally."

"Perhaps. He did say he was planning to spend Christmas with you and your parents."

"He did? For sure? That's wonderful! I never could get a solid commitment out of him."

"That's what he told me when I asked him to come to my place, so I suppose he's made up his mind. At least let's hope so."

"Then I'll wait and give him space," Whitney said, relieved to have learned that all was not lost.

"Maybe that is for the best, although there's nothing wrong with the whole, unvarnished truth, as I always say."

"Feel free to add me to your prayer list," Whitney said, bestowing a wistful smile on her companion. "And thanks for the good advice."

"It's only good if someone takes it," Coraline quipped. "If I don't have another chance to tell you, have a blessed Christmas."

"I will," Whitney said, getting to her feet and scooping up the tote. "You, too. Enjoy having your family home for the holidays." She winked before starting for the door. "And have fun with Mr. Randall."

"Please keep that information to yourself," Coraline cautioned. "We're not quite ready to announce anything."

"Wow, it's that serious?" Whitney gave her old friend a high five. "You go, girl!"

Coraline giggled. "Funny you should call me that. I feel younger since Robert and I started seeing each other than I have in many years."

"And I feel like Methuselah since I got interested in Josh," Whitney joked. "Only not half as smart as I should be at that age."

"Speaking of things biblical, are you going to the *Bethlehem* program at the church? Robert and I are. I really feel for those young actors, sitting out in this cold at night, and I want to show my support."

"I hadn't thought about it."

"Well, do. And why not ask Josh if he wants to go with you?"

Whitney's grin was widening. "Casually, of course."

"Of course." Coraline lifted a hand to wave. "Goodbye, dear. God bless you."

It was comforting to hear that blessing bestowed, particularly by an old friend. The principal could not be that bold with the current students, of course, but she managed to convey the same sense of caring and affection even when she didn't mention the Lord. It was in her expression and the way she related to everyone, even the smallest children.

Or the constantly misbehaving ones, Whitney thought, recalling her youth and how she had often wondered why Coraline was so kind to even the worst rule-breakers.

Now that she was older and had grown in her Christian faith she understood, of course. Miss Coraline was simply seeing the wounded souls beneath the rough exteriors and ministering to those rather than making snap judgments.

"That's what I should do in regard to Josh, too," Whitney told herself, chastened.

She glanced at the laptop lying beside her on the seat of her car as she started for home. Before she had driven half a block she had decided to stop at the Cozy Cup and ask Josh to take her to the Christmas pageant—before she changed her mind or lost her nerve.

The urge to see him again was what drove her. She knew that. But as long as *he* didn't catch on, all would be well.

She began to grin. "Besides, if he balks I can just tell him it was Coraline's idea."

Thankful that he'd had plenty of customers to serve as a distraction, Josh managed to keep functioning without being too angry with himself. What a bonehead move. He should never have kissed Whitney. What in the world had he been thinking?

"I wasn't thinking. That was the problem," he muttered.

The bells the florist had attached to his door wreath tinkled musically. Josh wiped his hand on his apron as he looked up. *Her! Again.* Was she trying to drive him crazy?

Remaining nonchalant he nodded in greeting. "Coffee?"

"Sure. Mocha, please."

Acting automatically, he slid a stainless steel pitcher beneath the frothing wand and turned it on while he prepared the chocolate flavor to add to the dark brown espresso trickling out of the machine.

When he turned around, Whitney was standing on the opposite side of the counter, a mere three feet away.

He set the mug in front of her and accepted the payment she offered, taking care to give her the proper change. "Still cold out?"

"Like Kansas in December," Whitney quipped. "And speaking of freezing weather, I wondered if you'd like to accompany me to the outdoor pageant at the community church tonight? The drama club is only going to present it a few times and we should all support them."

"I agree," Josh said, carefully wiping his already dry hands to give himself something to do. "Unfortunately, I've promised to help Matt tonight."

"Really? What's he up to?"

"Some of the kids and adults who worked on the home refurbishing project in the fall are going to go around stringing up Christmas lights on those same houses. Matt rooked me into helping."

"What a wonderful idea!"

"I thought so. Sorry I can't go to the church program with you."

He almost choked when Whitney smiled sweetly and said, "Not a problem. The drama is being presented one more night this week and twice next week. There's plenty of time to go. I just suggested tonight because that was when I planned to see it."

"Have a good time."

"Oh, I will. Next week. I can't believe Matt didn't ask me to string lights with his group. I helped on the painting and repair the same way you did."

"How well I remember." Josh made a face at her.

"Hey, it wasn't my fault. That ladder was rickety or something."

"Or something." He ran his hand over his dark auburn hair. "I didn't think I'd ever get all that white paint off me. It was even in my ears."

"If you'd been on your toes you'd have caught the paint can before it tipped over," she taunted.

"I was more concerned with keeping you from falling off that ladder. And you painted me from head to toe for my efforts." He couldn't help but smile remembering that day in September.

She laughed lightly. "At least there was no lasting harm done. Except maybe to your pride."

He watched her take a slow sip of her hot drink, then set it down. Her eyes widened. If she had been a cartoon character, a light bulb would have appeared above her head.

"I just had a great idea," Whitney told him.

Josh was not pleased. When it came to her ideas they too often included him, particularly of late.

Waiting for the trap to spring, the shoe to drop, the jack-in-the-box to pop up, Josh focused on her face. There was a glint in her eyes that did not bode well for him, and her soft lips were starting to lift in one of those hundred-watt smiles he'd gotten so used to seeing.

"Since I can catch the pageant next week there's no problem. I can help Matt tonight, too."

What could Josh say? *I don't want you there because I want you there too much?* Too bad his chaotic emotions could not be defragged and rebooted like a computer system.

Whitney laughed. "I wish you could see the look on your face. A person would think I'd just suggested we go rob a bank. It's community service. I do stuff like that all the time. Anybody in Bygones who's physically able would volunteer to do the same thing and you know it."

"Who are you trying to convince, me or yourself?"

She laughed again, softer this time. "You. I'm not trying to ruin your evening," Whitney vowed. "I'm just following up on a project we both worked on before. Isn't that why you told Matt you'd do it?"

"Of course it is."

"Well, then, you should be happy to have another set of hands participating. The more folks we have stringing lights, the faster we'll be done and in out of the cold."

"True. I've already invited everyone to gather here afterward to warm up and have a hot drink." He hesitated, then did the right thing. "You're welcome, too, of course."

"Thanks. Where are we meeting to begin?"

"At The Everything at six-thirty. Elwood and Velma have the lights for us, thanks to Miss Ann, and they promised slices of pizza as an incentive to show up. I figure that will bring lots of Matt's friends."

"Works for me, too." Whitney drained her cup and licked a bit of froth from her upper lip.

Josh felt his insides quaking as badly as if she'd leaped into his arms and planted a kiss smack in the middle of his mouth. Did she have any idea how her simplest actions were beginning to affect him? He doubted it. Whitney wasn't the type of woman to tease a man. She was simply being herself, with all her idiosyncrasies and the open innocence and gullibility of a newborn babe.

That was a big part of his dilemma. If he brought it to

her attention and asked her to stop, she'd know how much she was affecting him. And then what?

Josh sighed. Then, if she chose, she could become an even bigger problem, one he wasn't certain he could handle without making a fool of himself.

He already felt like one. Unbalanced when he was usually the voice of calm. Unsure when he was normally the man his employees sought out when they needed answers. Wavering in his decisions, his purpose, merely because of the influence of a pretty woman.

Well, that couldn't be helped. Not immediately, anyway. If he took one day at a time, a single encounter was not going to be enough to unhinge him.

At least he sincerely hoped it was not. He had graduated magna cum laude, winning academic honors greater than many other talented students. He had faced corporate bosses intent on taking over his business and had bested them. He had met foes in court over patents and had won in that arena, as well.

He was a winner. Always had been and always would be, God willing. So why was one special woman sending all his stability and self-assuredness out the window?

Because I care too much, Josh admitted ruefully. *I care way, way too much.*

Chapter Eleven

Whitney was so excited about the upcoming community project she arrived at The Everything a half hour early and decided to gas up her car there to kill time, then park it out of the way.

Going inside to pay for her fuel, she discovered that she wasn't the only one eager for pizza and good company. The Dills, Elwood and Velma, were there, of course, since they owned and ran the place. Both were in their mid-fifties, as far as Whitney could tell, considering Elwood's full, gray beard. The long-haired couple were self-styled hippies, showing enough tattoos to complete the image. In Velma's case, her excess weight made the one on her arm seem a trifle distorted and Whitney hated to imagine the inked images that might be hidden beneath the loose T-shirt and jeans currently covered by the woman's apron.

Matt and some teenage girls were standing off to one side. Most of the girls were busy texting on smartphones while one shared a paper plate of food with Matt and giggled every few seconds. Even Rory Liston had shown up, although since his arrest and community service sentence for vandalism, the teen had spent most of his time working to rehabilitate stray dogs at the animal shelter.

Lily and Tate Bronson had brought red-haired, eight-year-old Isabella, who was so enthusiastic she was practically jumping up and down. Seated with them were Melissa and Brian, from the Sweet Dreams Bakery.

Whitney smiled at Lily and nodded toward the little girl. "Looks like one of us is raring to go."

"Absolutely," the new stepmother replied. "I wish I had half her energy."

"Me, too."

Before Whitney had a chance to work her way to the counter she heard a bell tinkle. Patrick Fogerty was holding the door open for petite Gracie Wilson, his employee and fiancée. Gracie was gazing up at him as if he were the most amazing man in the entire world, which to her, he probably was.

In Whitney's opinion, however, no other guy even began to rival Josh Smith. Not in looks, or intellect, or sheer attractiveness, and that was only the beginning. If Josh changed his mind and didn't show up tonight she would still participate, but it wasn't going to be nearly as much fun without him.

Allison True, from the bookstore, was ahead of Whitney in line. "I'd like two slices, please," Allison said. "Sam's running a little late. He had to drop the twins at the babysitter's."

Whitney smiled. "It is pretty cold out there for toddlers. I'm surprised Tate brought Isabella."

"She's probably old enough to help," Allison said. "Keeping track of three-year-olds in the dark would be like trying to herd feral cats." She laughed lightly. "Particularly those two kids. What one doesn't think of, the other does. Rosie is usually pretty good but once Nicky gets her going it's every man for himself."

"Well, I think you're doing a wonderful job stepping into their mother's shoes. They needed stability," Whitney told her.

"Thanks." The slim, brown-haired young woman accepted her food and carried it aside to wait for her fiancé.

Whitney stepped up. "Hi, Velma. It's really sweet of you to offer to do this. Are you coming along when we go out to decorate?"

"'Fraid not. Can't leave when we're busy, which is most of the time now that Bygones is gettin' back on its feet." Her grin accented the puffy wrinkles at the corners of her eyes. "It's sure good to see."

"Very true." Whitney pointed to a glass-shielded warmer. "How about a slice of that pepperoni one? Do you have plenty?"

"Elwood's bakin' more right now. We're good."

"In that case, I'll take that kind. Are you sure I can't pay you for it?"

"Nope. It's on the house for anybody who's going out to decorate those old houses. It's gonna be such a blessing for those poor folks who can't do for themselves. Just like the repairs and painting were."

"I agree. Can I at least buy a soda?"

"Sure. Help yourself. Just tell Elwood what you took."

Whitney was balancing an enormous fountain drink and the paper plate of hot pizza when she heard the door again. Her heart stopped. So did her feet, and someone bumped into her from behind, causing her to stagger and nearly drop everything.

In an instant Josh was there. Steadying her, he took the soda in one hand, her elbow in the other, and guided her to the nearest table.

All Whitney could manage was a simple, "Thanks."

"You're welcome. Are you through wandering around or should I stay close by, just in case?"

She made a silly face. "I'm done. And that stumble was not my fault. Somebody pushed me."

"Right. Sit there and don't budge. I'll be back."

"I was on my way to pay Elwood for my soda."

"I'll take care of it. I'm sure he'd rather not have to mop the floor with this crowd milling around."

Although Josh had a valid point, Whitney still felt obligated to pay for her own drink. After all, the food had been free and Josh had often treated her to coffee or cocoa at his place. If she wasn't careful he was liable to think she made a habit of mooching.

She started to rise as she looked to see where he was. Not only was he staring at her, he scowled and pointed to her chair, mouthing, "Sit."

Whitney plopped back down. Laughter from behind caught her attention. She swiveled to see Chase Rollins. Vivian Duncan was with him and the chuckles were coming from her.

"Sorry," Vivian said with a smile. "I couldn't help it. You responded faster than the strays I've been training at the animal shelter."

Blushing, Whitney had to agree. "I suppose I should complain, but Josh just kept me from dumping my soda all over the floor so I guess I owe him one."

"I guess so. Are you going out with us to string lights tonight?"

"Uh-huh."

"Good. The more the merrier." Vivian lowered her voice and eyed the Cozy Cup owner in the distance. "How long have you and Josh been a couple? This is the first I've heard of it. Are you holding out on me?"

The warmth in her cheeks increased until Whitney figured she was probably as bright red as a Santa costume. "We're not a couple. We're just…I'm not sure what we are. Circumstances keep throwing us together."

"I'd call that a God-incidence, not a coincidence," Vivian said. "After all, look what happened to me." She held out her left hand to gaze fondly at her new engagement ring.

"I never thought I'd be a wife, let alone a mother, and all of a sudden the Lord sent me a baby to adopt."

"How is Theo?"

"Wonderful." Her expression softened. So did her voice. "He's a beautiful baby. So good and sweet." She glanced sidelong at Chase. "Just as wonderful as his future daddy."

"I'm happy for you," Whitney said honestly.

"You ought to try settling down. Love has changed my whole outlook on life."

"Because you've found the right man."

"Are you saying you haven't?" Once again she looked in Josh's direction. "Are you sure about that?"

Whitney shook her head. "I wish I knew. I really wish I knew."

The main part of the group left The Everything on foot since most of the houses they were planning to decorate were located close to downtown.

A few men, including Josh, toted stepladders. The brawniest teens brought the boxes of garlands and twinkle lights.

What surprised Josh most was the party atmosphere. Everybody seemed to be in high spirits, enough so that the mood was contagious. He had only agreed to participate because he wanted to support Matt's endeavors, particularly since the boy's widowed father was off being a missionary and the poor kid had been left with his grandparents.

Pastor and Mrs. Garman were nice people, they were simply from another generation. Besides, even though Josh had been an adult when his father had died, he still understood what it felt like to have only one parent. His mother, Susanna, had done her best, Josh knew, yet the emotional chasm between him and his late father had always made life difficult. And lonely.

Even now, trudging along in the slushy snow in the midst

of an amiable group such as this one, he felt isolated. Cut off. Perhaps that was his own fault for not taking others fully into his confidence. Patrick and Chase had both been very friendly in the months since they'd all arrived in Bygones. Josh could have let them into his private life if he'd wanted to. But he had not.

And now? Now, so much time had passed that he wondered if anyone in town was going to speak to him after they learned who he really was and why he had come. When Coraline had suggested he consider confessing publicly, his main concern had been how Whitney might take it. Now that he'd had more time to mull it over, he was beginning to realize that she was not going to be the only one who would be upset. Literally everyone he had met could turn against him. In a heartbeat.

A voice at his elbow jarred him.

"You look like somebody just ran over your dog," Whitney said.

"I don't have a dog."

"It's a country expression, Josh. What's wrong? Is the ladder too heavy?"

He huffed. "No. Life gets that way sometimes, though. Heavy, I mean."

"Isn't your shop making money? All the rest of the new businesses are starting to show a nice profit."

"I'm doing okay."

"Then what's going on? If you looked any more dumpy, we'd have to get you a T-shirt like Allison had on last week. It said 'Bah! Humbug!'" She stopped speaking although she continued to keep pace.

Josh knew she was giving him a perfect opportunity to tell her what was really bothering him. Did he dare open up a little? Perhaps, but not in a crowd like this. And certainly not when his hands were full.

"You get the shirt, I'll think about wearing it," he said. "How are your folks?"

"Fine. Dad says thanks for fixing his toy with all those whistles and bells. And Mom wanted me to tell you we're eating our big meal at one on Christmas day."

"Okay. Can I bring anything?"

"You're coming? Really? When Coraline told me you'd said you were, I could hardly believe it."

"If I'm still invited, I'll be there," he said flatly. "You and I should have a talk before that, though. I need to share some important news with you."

"About the movie? I've already started to write the announcement for you but I will need more particulars, like show time and whether you're giving out tickets early. Things like that."

"Right."

To Josh's relief their group was approaching one of the homes they'd worked on before. Others knocked on the door to announce their arrival while the teens began to pull strings of lights out of boxes and untangle them.

"Just do the porches and whatever else is easy to reach," Patrick announced. "We don't want to drive a lot of nails or put staples into the eaves. In other words, keep it simple, folks."

Simple? Josh snorted in self-disgust. Nothing had been simple or even halfway normal since he'd started spending time with Whitney—and loving it—almost every day. He was going to have to tell her something very soon. His gut was already churning from contemplating what he should or shouldn't say and his pulse kept running away whenever she got too close.

At that moment she was helping Matt and his friends straighten out the light strings and laughing as if blissfully happy. That was the way Josh liked to see her. Filled with joy and living life to the fullest.

Once he revealed more about himself, would it steal her serenity, shake her faith in him and make her question everything he'd ever told her? If only he could look into the future.

God can, he heard his heart say. *Trust Him.*

Josh's reaction to that thought was one of awe. He handed off the ladder, stepped around the trunk of a large elm for privacy, closed his eyes, and whispered, "Father, help me do the right thing the right way. Please. I don't know a lot about the Bible yet but I knew enough to put my whole life in Your hands. Can You show me more? Help me to make Whitney understand? Really understand. Anything but hate me. Please, Lord?"

When he circled the tree to rejoin the group of amateur decorators he ran smack into the very woman he'd been praying about.

Looking startled at first, then smiling, she rested her gloved palms on his chest while his arms instinctively encircled her.

"*There* you are," Whitney said. "I wondered where you'd gone. We need a tall guy on the end by the driveway."

Josh didn't reply. Nor did he release her immediately. He saw her eyes widen and her lips part. Clouds of their frozen breath mingled between them. Was she silently asking for another kiss? He wanted to think so. She certainly wasn't pushing him away.

He cocked his head left and leaned closer.

Whitney moved her face ever so slightly the opposite direction.

They were so close now it was as if their kiss was inevitable. He hesitated only a moment.

"Hey, Smith," a male voice shouted from the house. "You gonna help us or not?"

Whitney jumped and Josh leaped back as if someone had set off a taser between them.

She giggled nervously. "Oops."

Josh was less than thrilled about the man's timing, although if he were honest with himself, the summons had probably been for the best.

"Yeah, I'm coming," he shouted back.

Without saying another word, he left Whitney standing next to the elm and jogged through the trampled snow toward the house. Was he crazy? Seriously thinking of kissing her again was bad enough without actually doing it in public.

Once the truth about him was known, he'd have to be very diligent in making sure no one blamed her or assumed she had been part of the plot. After he'd sold the Cozy Cup and left town, he didn't want Whitney to suffer for having known him.

The concept of leaving Bygones for keeps wasn't new, yet this time it hit him like a sucker punch. He was going to miss living here. He was going to miss these special people and their friendships.

And he'd especially miss a certain reporter who had inched her way into his life, and into his heart, in a way he had never dreamed possible. He had no doubt that long after he had forgotten most of the folks he'd met in the sleepy little town, Whitney Leigh would still be a bright star, a supernova in his most vivid and fond memories.

Whitney pressed her gloved hands over her mouth and cheeks as she watched Josh walk away. Her heart was about to pound out of her chest and there was a definite lack of oxygen in the moist, night air.

He'd wanted to kiss her in spite of vowing it would never happen again. She *knew* he had. Certainly he must have sensed her willingness. By morning, half the town would know they had been embracing, so what difference would it have made if he had given in and kissed her? Was she so undesirable? He definitely didn't act as though he felt that way.

The thing that really galled her was his unexplained reticence. They were two adults, not a couple of teens caught up in the throes of a hormone storm. There had been few young men in her life to begin with, and none had affected her nearly as strongly as Josh Smith did.

Miss Coraline had suggested frankness. Whitney toyed with the silly notion of tying him to that tree so he'd have to listen, then giving him a piece of her mind. She wouldn't, of course, but fantasizing about it helped her calm down.

"He said we needed to talk," Whitney muttered, going to the opposite end of the porch from where Josh was working. "Well, I'm going to talk all right. And, one way or another, I'm going to find out why he's playing so hard to get."

Assuming he's playing and not deathly serious, she mused. If he was truly trying to keep her at arms' length, she had a feeling she was not going to like his responses to her confession that she was crazy about him.

Chapter Twelve

If Josh had been trying his best to stick close to Whitney he could not have run into her any more often. When he moved the ladder and climbed, there she was to hand him things. When he backed off to survey their work, she just happened to be doing the same. And when he and a few others proceeded to another house, she tagged along.

It wasn't overt pursuit. At least he didn't think it was. Her nearness seemed to be half due to his heightened awareness of her and half because they were doing the same job. If he assessed the entire situation logically, it was clear that he was just as close to most of the others as he was to Whitney. But it was she, alone, who captured his full attention.

Her smile was brilliant. Her eyes twinkled like the brightest Christmas lights. Her cheeks were rosy from the cold and her laugh...Josh didn't think he'd ever tire of hearing her light, uplifting laugh. It stood out above everyone else's the same way her personality did.

"We're running out of lights," Matt declared loudly. "I'll run back and see if Coach Franklin's group has extras."

Josh would have volunteered to go if the teen hadn't waited until he was at the top of a ladder to announce the decision. Watching Matt jog away he was struck by how the other young people were accompanying him. Not only that, since offshoots of the original group had gone their separate ways as well, Josh was now left with only one helper. Whitney Leigh.

She stood at the base of the ladder, steadying it on the uneven ground. "You may as well come down. That's the last string we have."

"How about garlands? Are we out of those, too?"

"Afraid so. I think we put too much of everything on the first few houses we did."

He started to back down the ladder. "Well, then we'll have to see if we can come up with more decorations later. I can come back and finish up some evening after work."

"The kids should do it. School vacation starts soon and they're better off with a constructive outlet for all their energy." Whitney grinned at him. "Besides playing video games, I mean."

"There is nothing wrong with playing on a computer as long as I've approved the games and they don't play exclusive of everything else. I time them and limit their usage, within reason."

She laughed. "You can't fool me, Smith. You just want to play, too, and sometimes you have to kick the kids out so you can."

He was chuckling as he finished descending and stopped beside her. "Not really. I have my own gaming and computing stations in my apartment."

"Is that why you didn't want Matt to go up there?"

"Who told you that?"

"He did." Whitney shook her head. "Really, Josh, he's just a kid. There was no need to get upset. I'm sure he didn't mean to bother you."

"I never said he did. I just don't like company when I'm..."

"When you're what? Planning a bank heist or hacking into some secret site? Give me a break." She began to blush. "You aren't one of those guys who looks at naughty pictures, are you?"

"Of *course* not. I can't believe you'd even ask."

"Then what's the big secret? Did you forget to do your laundry or leave dirty dishes in the sink?"

"Something like that." He cupped the elbow of her coat and guided her toward the street. "Come on. Let's go find those kids. If they didn't locate more lights we'll ask Patrick to pick up the ladders in his truck so we don't have to carry them all the way back."

"Then what?"

"Then, I'll head to the Cozy Cup and keep my promise to provide hot chocolate for the volunteers."

"Mind if I tag along now instead of coming over later?"

He almost laughed at himself when he managed to say, "I guess it would be okay." In his heart, there was nobody he wanted to treat more than the cute reporter.

Even if she could be a real pain sometimes.

Make that *all* the time.

The camaraderie of everyone gathered in the coffee shop was palpable, as if the overall joy of the season permeated everything. Josh was being the perfect host, with Matt's help, whenever the teen managed to stop flirting with the youngest True sister, Amy.

Because of the time change in the fall, it had gotten dark early. When Whitney checked her watch she was astounded to see that it was nearly nine. "How time flies when you're having fun."

And she was enjoying herself. Sort of. Normally, she would not have minded being part of such an amiable crowd. In this case, however, she wondered how long she'd have to wait to get the chance to speak to Josh privately. That possibility was not looking promising.

Finally she approached the counter.

"Need a refill?" he asked.

"No, thanks. I've had enough." She covered a yawn. "Sorry. It's been a long day. I just wanted to tell you how much we all appreciate your hospitality."

"Thanks. I try."

Although she'd intended to keep their conversation casual, she realized that her personal concerns might be dulling her overall sense of contentment when she asked, "So, are we still on for next week?"

The puzzlement on his face amused her and boosted her mood. Her smile broadened naturally. "For the outdoor pageant. Remember? You said you couldn't go tonight because of this decorating project."

"I don't recall promising to go later."

"It was implied," Whitney said flatly. "*Bethlehem* is a walk-through experience. The kids will play their parts over and over again when the guides bring a new group to see the crèche. They're really cute. Some are actually very talented."

"I'm sure they are."

She could almost see the wheels turning in his brain as he searched for a valid excuse to turn her down.

Finally, Josh shrugged. "Okay. What time?"

"The last performance nights are Friday and Saturday. They open at six. The sooner we get there, the less we'll freeze." She shivered and folded her arms across her chest. "Makes me cold just thinking about it. I remember one year, when I was playing an angel, it actually snowed on us."

"No wonder you're so keen on going." His grin was a pleasant change from the sober looks he'd been giving her. "An angel, huh? Definitely not typecasting."

"I wanted to play Mary, but that part was already taken so I settled for what I could get. My only other option was to wear fake fur and pretend I was a camel."

As she had hoped, her quip made him laugh softly. The

welcome sound sent tingles up and down her spine and made her insides quiver. Either that, or the pizza from The Everything had suddenly given her indigestion.

Whitney, she told herself, *you are hopeless. You'd rather credit indigestion for your unsettled feelings than consider that you're so crazy about Josh Smith you can hardly stand it.*

That conclusion was correct, of course. She was terribly off-balance. Did that mean she'd actually fallen in love with the man, or was she merely suffering from a childish infatuation that would soon fade? She had no idea. Nor did she know how to tell the difference. It wasn't as if she made a habit of falling for any man who happened to be nice to her.

Besides, she reminded herself, Josh did not seem to be trying to court her. On the contrary, he was so reticent she often suspected he was putting her off rather than attempting to get to know her better.

Well, so be it. She was no bashful teen. And she was not going to behave like Amy True, giggling at everything Matt said as if he were the cleverest person she'd ever met.

Younger women might try to remake themselves into someone they thought would please the man in whom they were interested. Whitney was not going to fall into that trap. She was going to be totally herself. Faithful to her instincts and freely demonstrating her slightly eccentric personality. That way, if Josh did finally admit he was interested in her, she'd know it was in spite of everything, not because she had misrepresented herself in order to be more attractive to him.

"I'll be here before you close next Saturday," Whitney told him. "Be sure you have a warm jacket. A scarf or a hat wouldn't hurt, either. If the wind is blowing you'll need them."

Bending, he pulled a red baseball cap from beneath the counter and slapped it on his head. "Like this?"

The logo stenciled on the front was for The Fixer-Upper, Patrick Fogerty's hardware store. "I take it that was free."

"Of course. Gotta help advertise other businesses."

Josh left the hat in place, pulling on the brim to bring it lower over his eyes before peering out at her. "Do you like it?"

"At least it fits the traditional colors of the season," she told him with a wave and a smile. "Thanks again for the cocoa. See you in church tomorrow."

Whitney didn't stop grinning until she reached her car and climbed in. Josh was going to go to the pageant with her! He hadn't acted as if he was very enthused but she couldn't be choosy when it came to drawing him out.

In retrospect, she realized he'd always remained slightly aloof in spite of participating in town meetings and finally deciding to attend church. He wasn't a mixer the way she was. He was basically an outsider who, instead of opening up the way the other new business people had, remained reclusive.

Josh had every right to behave that way, she reasoned. Yet there seemed to be a lonesomeness about him that called to her; it touched a tender place in her heart and insisted that she be the one who showed him how much he was missing.

And they were going to be together again at least twice. First in church, then again at the pageant. Things were definitely looking up. She could hardly wait.

The following week was one of the longest Josh had ever experienced. He'd skipped church on Sunday, only to find Whitney knocking on his door by twelve-thirty to ask if he was ill and offer to bring him chicken soup.

Although his excuse of thinking he was coming down with a cold had been iffy, she'd seemed to accept it at the time. She had, however, returned for coffee at least twice a day since then and had continually inquired about his health, almost going so far as insinuating that his illness had been a sham.

Now that it was Saturday evening, he knew she'd had plenty of opportunities to decide he was well enough to keep their date, as promised, and he had to force himself to stop watching the clock and pacing while he waited for her to arrive.

There she was! The sight of Whitney's approach, viewed through the frosty window, did funny things to his pulse. As recently as a few months ago, if anyone had told him he was going to lose his heart to a nosy reporter in a backwater Kansas town like Bygones, he would have insisted it was impossible.

As Pastor Garman was fond of saying, however, nothing is impossible with God. Was that what was happening? Josh wondered. Was all this some unbelievable, divine plan for his life? Because if it was, it was certainly nothing like the way he had envisioned his future before coming here.

For the first time since his decision to follow Jesus and join the church, Josh began to wonder just how far back God's plans for him might go? If, as the Bible said, God had known him before he was even born, then perhaps his altruism in regard to the struggling old town had been predictable.

Granted, he could still make enough mistakes to thwart any good heavenly influence. That was scripturally clear. So the question then became, What did God want and was it the same thing he, himself, wanted?

Was he willing to take the chance of confessing everything and accept whatever Whitney said and did as a result? Was it possible she might be so angry and disillusioned she'd never speak to him again? The thought of that happening was so depressing it hit him like a punch in the stomach.

The bells on the door tinkled musically. The wreath swung slightly as Whitney swept through. She was all smiles.

Allowing himself to reflect the same elation, he grinned and waved. "Hi. You're early."

"I didn't want to leave my car out in the cold and take a chance on damage to the top, so I walked over. I didn't know how long that would take me in this weather. I didn't want you to think I'd stood you up."

"Never." Josh chuckled low. "After all the trouble you took to railroad me into agreeing to go with you, I knew you'd show up."

"Of course." She made a silly face at him, her eyes sparkling like polished emeralds. "My dad often says he hears train whistles when Mom and I arrange an outing that includes him. Now, of course, he can get out of doing just about anything if he blames his sore knee."

"My knees are fine," Josh told her, knowing he was grinning inanely and not caring.

"And your cold is gone?"

"Like I was never sick." Untying his apron he wadded it into a ball and tossed it into a laundry basket behind the curtain to his workroom. "Matt's agreed to close up for me tonight so we can get going early. Like you said, it's going to be really cold later."

"Wonderful." She pointed at the counter as if she could see through it. "Still got that classy hat?"

"Of course. I wouldn't want to be taken for a foreigner."

"That is part of the usual dress code around here. Although a feed company hat would make you look more like a real farmer."

"When I was a kid I wanted to be a cowboy. I suppose this is about as close as I'll ever get."

Whitney giggled. "Probably. Next time I pay a call on

a feed mill to ask them to advertise in the *Gazette,* I'll see if I can get you one of their hats."

"Thanks. I think." He slipped his jacket on and zipped it, then squared the red baseball cap on his head, running his hand down the back of his neck. "Feels like I need a haircut."

"You're fine. The first time I saw you, you had one of those fancy Hollywood haircuts and it made you look out of place in Bygones."

"I'm better now?" He scrubbed a palm over his cheek. "Do I need to shave again before we go? I wouldn't want to embarrass you."

"You're fine. Wonderful," Whitney said, taking his arm. "Dad always claims a day's growth of whiskers keeps his face warmer in the winter." She laughed again. "Of course, it's possible that's just a good excuse to skip shaving once in a while."

"Your father is a real character," Josh said. "I liked him. A lot. And your mother."

"Good. They thought you were okay, too, especially after all the wonders you performed on Dad's laptop. I still can't believe your friend hasn't marketed his idea. He'd make a fortune."

"Maybe someday," Josh said, wondering if this was the opening he'd prayed for. "I imagine it would be lucrative."

"Well, don't you worry about things like that," Whitney said as he led the way to the white van he always drove and held the passenger side door for her. "I'm not the kind who judges a person by his checkbook. As a matter of fact, I think too much money can be a real trial. People who live the way you and I do are much happier and more content, don't you think?"

Josh circled and slid behind the wheel before answering. "Oh, I don't know. Money is just a tool. It's no different than this van. If I drive recklessly I may get hurt or hurt someone else. But if I'm careful, it's not at all dangerous."

She was shaking her head as she fastened her seatbelt. "Uh-uh. Bad analogy. The problem is the sense of absolute power that rich folks get. They think they can do anything if they're wealthy. They can lie and cheat and behave abominably as long as their bank accounts are full enough to bail them out of trouble."

"Not everyone is like that." He paused for effect. "Look at the guy you call Mr. Moneybags. He's doing good, isn't he?"

"Maybe. Maybe not."

When Josh glanced over at her she was frowning and her lips were pressed into a thin line. "What do you mean?"

"It's the secrecy that bothers me most," Whitney said. "If there's nothing for him—or her—to hide, then why be so mysterious?"

Before he had a chance to come up with a plausible reply she added, "I think I may have figured out who it is."

His hands tightened on the wheel. Was she about to call his bluff? "Really?"

"Uh-huh," Whitney said, sounding excited. "I think it's Robert Randall."

Josh felt as if all the air had suddenly left his lungs and deflated him like a balloon. "Randall? Why him?"

"Because he's the only one I know with that kind of cash, although there are a few holes in my theory. He claimed he was almost bankrupt when he closed the plant and laid everybody off. If he was fibbing, it's going to kill Miss Coraline when she finds out."

"Coraline Connolly? My SOS mentor?"

"Yes." Whitney lowered her voice and cupped a hand around one side of her mouth despite the fact that they were inside the van where no one could overhear. "She and Robert have been dating."

"Well, well." He gave her time to say more. When she didn't, he asked, "If they're so fond of each other, why would she doubt that his motives were honorable?"

"A lie is a lie," Whitney said flatly. "If he cared about her the way she thinks he does, he'd have confided in her long ago." She brightened. "Hey! Maybe he did and she's in on the whole thing. The last couple of times I talked to her, I got the impression she knew more than she was letting on. When she wouldn't show me the original paperwork for the grants, she really set off my internal alarms."

"Before you go casting blame and make a mistake, maybe it would be a good idea to bide your time."

"Oh, I will, I will. Which reminds me. I managed to find one of the copies she passed out when this Main Street project began. It had a different email address on it. You can help me figure out who that one belongs to."

"I told you. I'm not a hacker."

She sent him a disgruntled look. "Oh, okay. You're probably right about the legalities and I wouldn't want to break the law. Are you sure you can't just *bend* it a little?"

Not if I want to keep my top-secret clearance to provide essential defense programs to the U.S. government, Josh thought.

All he said was, "Does Pastor Garman know you're a wannabe sinner?"

Whitney giggled. "No. And don't you dare tell him."

Chapter Thirteen

"Park behind the church," Whitney said, pointing. "There should be room back there."

"I can't believe all these cars and pickup trucks. Does the pageant always draw such a big crowd?"

"Usually. Even in bad weather most of the town turns out. I love to come."

"Still remembering your angel wings?"

"Something like that. If you try, you may find yourself imagining being there when this actually happened, although scholars disagree about many of the details."

"Seasons and travel times for the Magi, you mean?"

Whitney nodded, impressed that he would make a special effort to study Christ's birth. "You've been doing your homework."

"I figured I should know all I could, particularly if I was going to have to defend my faith."

"Have you had to?" It gave her a sense of relief when he shook his head and said, "No. Not yet."

"Well, I suppose you will. I have a terrible time explaining why I believe the way I do. There are times when I envy children their simple faith. Adults tend to muddy the waters with too much logic."

"I totally agree."

She chuckled. “That’s a surprise. I’ve never known anybody more rational than you are.”

“Is that a compliment?” Josh asked as he wheeled into an empty parking space.

“I’m reserving judgment,” Whitney said. She climbed out before he could circle the van and open her door for her. It wasn’t that she didn’t want him to exhibit good manners, she simply wanted to exert her independence.

Josh joined her. “Okay. Where do we go first?”

“Inside the church to get a guide and join a group.”

Leading the way, she couldn’t help feeling elated. Not only was she among old friends, Josh was with her.

As he followed he said, “I was kind of hoping you and I would have some private time. It seems like we’re only together when there are a gazillion other people around.”

“I’ve been thinking about that,” Whitney told him. “My folks haven’t done any decorating this year. What do you think about us picking up a tree and a pizza and taking it to my house as a surprise for them after we finish here?”

Whitney, who was used to jumping at chances for fun, thought Josh was taking an inordinately long time to decide. She supposed it was only a second or two but it seemed like ages.

When he finally said, “Okay. Sounds good to me,” she almost cheered.

Slipping her hand through the crook of his elbow she urged him forward. “Wonderful! Come on. Let’s see who got to play the angels this year.”

“Probably some kids who are usually in trouble,” he quipped. “Just the way I picture you as a child.”

She had to laugh. “You are getting to know me far too well, Mr. Smith.”

When Josh replied with, “Not nearly as well as I’d like to know you,” Whitney’s breath caught, her insides quivering.

Make up your mind, she lectured herself cynically. *Ei-*

ther you want him to get serious about you, or you don't. You can't have it both ways.

No, she couldn't. But that didn't mean she wasn't scared. Her life had been settled and predictable until she'd started to care for Josh so much. If their relationship progressed and grew as intense as the ones she'd been writing about lately, everything would change. It would have to.

Worried, she wondered if she was merely caught up by the epidemic of romances that had filled Bygones in the past six months. Was her mind playing tricks on her? Maybe leading her to imagine love where there was none?

There was only one sensible option. She had to let this relationship develop and see where it took her, because there was no way she was going to walk away from Josh Smith after what he had just said.

Sensing Whitney's reticence, Josh satisfied himself with her company and remained silent as they made their way to the makeshift city of Bethlehem, portrayed as it was over two thousand years ago. The story the guide was telling was obviously a memorized speech but the man delivered it well.

Teens and adults dressed as Roman soldiers accosted the group on the trail as if they were true pilgrims on their way to pay their taxes to Caesar Augustus.

Along the make-believe road were small recreations of huts that represented villages, with occupants who were clad in the robes typical of so long ago. Each place had its communal fire burning inside a rock ring, providing both atmosphere and warmth to the actors.

"I hope they have jackets and boots under those loose robes," Josh whispered to Whitney. "This is no desert."

"I'm sure they're warm enough," she replied. "When I played an angel my mother insisted I wear three layers of clothes. I kept insisting that angels didn't get cold."

"Sounds like you."

"Thanks, I think." She laid a finger across her lips. "Shush. We're almost there."

Passing through wooden gates, the party was told they were entering Bethlehem. The notes of heralding trumpets sounded over loudspeakers. A spotlight illuminated a group of angels, complete with halos and wings, as one announced the birth of the Savior.

Then, there was the manger scene. Actors bowed before the baby king in the manger and pronounced him Lord while the spectators watched.

Josh felt Whitney take his hand.

"You're not wearing gloves," she said. "Are you warm enough?"

"I'm fine."

He knew this was not the time to tell her how her mere presence warmed him all the way to his heart. That would come later, after he had bared his soul and judged her reaction.

Diverting his attention on purpose, he made a subtle gesture with his free hand. "Nice angel. Was that your part?"

"No. I was one of the smaller ones around the manger. Only my arms kept getting really tired." She grinned up at him. "Mom has a photo of me. I look as if I'm about to collapse and fall asleep on top of baby Jesus."

Josh gave a quiet laugh. "Cute."

"I was. At least that's what everybody said then."

"You're still not bad," he gibed, hoping she'd accept a compliment that wasn't too flowery. The last thing he wanted to do was scare her away before he had a chance to confess his love.

It *was* that, wasn't it? He did love Whitney. Being unable to imagine any future without her in it was a sure sign; one he had battled against for weeks.

How would that fit in with his business? he wondered.

He supposed he could take Coraline's advice and think seriously about relocating the headquarters of Barton Technologies. Or, he could continue to handle things the way he had been, by telecommuting and making occasional trips back up to St. Louis. Anything was possible. He'd make it work. For Whitney.

The Magi were arriving, shooing real sheep out of the way and leading a motley group of camels. Josh had to smile. "There's your other costume choice, right?"

"Right. I figured I'd look better with a halo and wings."

"Absolutely." He gave her hand an affectionate squeeze as the narrative continued.

The wise men knelt before the baby and presented their gifts. One of the foil and paper crowns slipped as they did so and tumbled into the manger. The girl playing Mary snatched it off her doll and thrust it at the hapless boy, beating him with it as if he'd purposely harmed her make-believe baby.

Titters erupted from the crowd, including Whitney. The narrator never missed a beat. He mentioned the shepherds, who were present but having no luck keeping their actual sheep from nibbling the hay that was part of the scenery. Thankfully, one was tethered so the others didn't stray far from it.

Finally, it was time for the journey into exile in flight from Herod's murderous edict. Everyone rose. Joseph took the halter of the lone donkey and waited while shepherds and Magi helped the girl playing Mary onto its back. All was set for the grand finale. The group started to move off very solemnly—until Mary realized something was amiss.

The audience had seen the error, of course, and there was an undercurrent of whispers and giggles passing among them. In the background, the adult supervisor was waving her arms frantically and trying to signal the earnest children.

Josh had to grit his teeth to keep from erupting in laughter when the girl squealed, slid off the donkey, left all the other players, and hurried back to the manger.

All would have been well if she had simply cradled the doll at that point. She didn't. She grabbed the pretend baby by its foot and rushed to resume her place in the company of child actors, trailing swaddling and scattering straw to mark her path.

That was all the crowd could take and still remain solemn and respectful. Funny was funny, no matter what the circumstances. And once the peals of laughter began they multiplied like the sands of the desert the players were supposed to be crossing.

Josh could see many shoulders shaking with mirth. Even the play's director had lost her cool. The poor, red-faced woman had her hands clapped over her mouth to mute her giggles and tears were streaming down her cheeks as she laughed along with nearly everyone else.

Leaning to speak softly to Whitney, Josh said, "Well, you told me it would be memorable."

She was laughing so hard she had trouble talking. "No… kidding!"

"I'm glad the real Mary took better care of her special baby."

Recovering, Whitney nodded. "It must have been a heavy burden, knowing who He was and why He'd been born. I can't imagine."

"You know, if you consider the problems we all think we have now, ours are nothing." He slipped an arm around her shoulders as the play concluded and the actors regrouped for their next performance.

"You're right, of course. I hadn't made the comparison before. Not really."

"So, what now?" Josh asked. "Do you still want to pick up a tree and a pizza?"

"If you're up for it."

"I am. And I'm starving. How far do we have to go to find a tree?"

"Not far. Last time I looked, there were still some stacked outside the Hometown Grocery the mayor's wife manages. If we're not too fussy, one of those should do."

"It's up to you," he replied. "I've never bought a dead tree before."

Whitney made a pouting face at him. "What a description. Don't tell me your parents never took you along when they shopped for one."

"They might have, if they'd decorated their house for the holidays themselves. My father always hired a professional decorator who put up a fake, white tree and accented it with plain, red ornaments. As far as my dad was concerned, pine needles scattered all over the carpet were unacceptable."

"Your mother went along with that?"

"You had to know my dad," Josh said, sobering. "He was pretty authoritarian."

"I'm beginning to think that's an understatement. You must have had a really odd childhood."

"I never thought so." He shrugged. "Like I've said before, you can't miss what you've never had."

"I suppose not." They had passed the door to the church and were headed for the parking area when Whitney remarked, "You said you wanted to talk to me about something?"

"Later." The importance of their planned conversation weighed on his conscience. "Let's go get that tree before they're all gone and then pick up a pizza at The Everything."

"Okay," Whitney said, climbing into the passenger side of the van while he held the door. "But I should warn you. I don't have a lot of patience. I'm liable to get really testy if you keep me waiting too long."

"I'll take my chances," he said with a slight smile as he closed the door.

Circling the van he clenched his jaw and his fists. He would tell her, he vowed. *Tonight.* He would take her aside and confess his role in the funding of the Save Our Streets project.

But he wouldn't say anything until after they'd spent one more blissful evening together. It might be his last chance to feel as if he were a part of a loving family. As if he and Whitney truly belonged together.

If she had ever had more fun decorating a Christmas tree, Whitney couldn't remember when. Not only were her parents surprised and thrilled to have a tree, even this close to Christmas, they were behaving as if they accepted Josh completely. It was wonderful to share her blessings with someone like him. Someone who had missed out on this kind of cheerful gathering his whole life.

On one of her forays into the kitchen for soda refills, Whitney had had a chance to tell Betty a little about his background.

"No real holiday celebrations at all? That's unbelievable," her mother had said.

"I know. Isn't it sad? I mean for his mom, too. I didn't have a chance to ask him much about her but I gather she's not poor. Not if she can afford a cruise."

"They aren't that expensive," Betty countered. "If friends of hers are also going, maybe they got a reduced rate. I'm just glad to hear she's not sitting home alone."

"Yeah, me, too. And that Josh will feel free to come here that day."

"You really like him, don't you, honey?"

"Uh-huh."

Betty sighed. "Well, that's not surprising. You were always hauling home injured birds and lost puppies. Come to think of it, I'm surprised you didn't get interested in that man who runs the pet store."

"Chase Rollins? Not my type. Besides, he has a fiancée. He and Vivian Duncan are planning to get married. You remember her from the bookstore, don't you?"

"And before that. I think she was a year or so ahead of you in school, wasn't she? A pretty little thing. Red-haired, if I recall."

"It's dark, like auburn," Whitney said, rolling her eyes. "She's gorgeous."

"So are you, dear."

"Spoken like my mother." She gave a sharp laugh and pushed her glasses up her nose out of habit. "Honestly, do you think these frames are ugly?"

"Of course not. They make you look—studious."

"That's fine if I want to impress Ed at the *Gazette*. How about anybody else? Are they too heavy? Do they make me look frumpy?"

"I wouldn't go that far," Betty said kindly. "They can seem a bit overwhelming sometimes, especially if I'm trying to see your pretty green eyes."

Whitney removed the glasses and laid them aside on the kitchen counter. "Josh's eyes are green, too. Sort of, anyway. I guess you'd say they're more hazel than green. It kind of depends on his mood and the lighting."

"Uh-huh." Betty handed her two of the four refilled glasses. "Here you go. The one with the snowman picture is Josh's. Yours is the angel."

"Of course it is." Whitney brightened and began to grin. "You should have seen the church pageant tonight. There wasn't a dry eye in the crowd."

"Because it was so moving?"

Whitney giggled. "Nope. Just the opposite. Come on. Let's go back to the guys and Josh can tell you all about it."

Color rose to redden her cheeks as she added, "And

later, when we can be alone, he wants to have a serious talk with me." The warmth of her cheeks made her feel as if she were glowing.

"Oh, my..."

"My thoughts *exactly,*" Whitney said. "I can hardly wait."

Chapter Fourteen

As far as Josh was concerned, the evening was marching along at the speed of a snail. A tired snail. He managed to hold up his end of most of the conversations except where the others referenced townspeople whom he had not met, such as those from the past. It was his fondest wish that no one would bring up his mother. Since she had left Bygones as a teen and made the city of St. Louis her permanent home, he figured he was pretty safe.

Mrs. Leigh had put out paper plates for the pizza and since there were no cooking pans, either, she was through straightening up the kitchen in no time and had returned to watch the tree trimming.

"Unfortunately," Josh muttered to himself as he nested the empty ornament boxes for storage until they were needed again. He needed to talk to Whitney alone.

Whitney was busy draping tinsel over the ornaments and lights on the Christmas tree they'd selected. It had one excellent side and one not so good, so they had placed it in a corner of the cozy living room where it would stand out without being in the way and also not be in contact with curtains that might be flammable. Now that he'd seen what it was like to bring such an awkward item into the house and bedeck it with so much color and sparkle, he could definitely see why his late father had not encouraged the family to take up the custom themselves. Practically speaking, it was a waste of time and money.

And yet, Whitney seemed enchanted by it. Her joy was almost palpable as she continued to adjust the drape of the garlands and add a shiny ornament here and there. In that respect his father had been wrong, he decided, surprising himself. Carpets could always be vacuumed. Anything that brought happiness into a home should never be banned, not even if it caused a terrible mess.

That thought was still lingering when Whitney asked such an unexpected question he wondered for an instant if she had sensed that he was reminiscing.

"What gift did you ask for when you were little that you never got?" She giggled. "I never got my pony."

"And I never got a dog," he replied wistfully. "My mother was okay with it but my dad insisted it would get the house dirty."

"I didn't have the option of bringing a pony into the house," she said, laughing as if she hadn't noticed how serious he'd become. "Both my parents kept telling me we didn't have room for horses in the yard."

"Did you live in this same house while you were growing up?"

Whitney nodded. "Uh-huh. We've never lived anywhere else. It's comfortable, and when Dad was able he kept up the repairs so it never seemed old." She sighed. "It is, I suppose. I just never thought of it that way until now."

"I was kind of surprised to learn you still lived at home."

She shrugged. "Where else would I want to go? I pay a little rent, of course, to help out, but I see no reason to move into an apartment when I'm perfectly comfortable here. Besides, Mom needs help sometimes, so it works out for all of us, particularly since Dad's surgery."

"Don't they have visiting nurse services around here?"

"Not that I know of. They probably do up in Manhattan but I doubt a nurse would come this far, particularly on a regular basis. In case you haven't noticed, Bygones is kind of in the boonies."

"I noticed." He finished stacking the empty ornament boxes on a chair and glanced at her parents. Betty was engrossed in a paperback and J.T. was snoring in his recliner, feet elevated. "Can we go somewhere private to talk?"

Whitney froze, her arm raised and holding a handful of crinkly plastic tinsel. It only took her an instant to fling the whole silvery mass at the tree where it landed halfway up like a distorted, miniature octopus with sparkling tentacles.

Josh had to laugh. "What kind of system is that?"

"Mine." She grabbed his hand. "Let's go into the kitchen. I'd normally suggest the porch swing but we'd freeze out there this time of year."

Betty looked up as they passed, hand in hand. "There's more pizza in the fridge if you're still hungry. And you left your eyeglasses on the counter if you're looking for them, honey."

He squeezed Whitney's fingers. "I noticed you weren't wearing them tonight. I thought you couldn't see without your glasses."

"I see well enough to decorate a tree. I could practically do that in my sleep."

"You can see my face clearly, can't you?" They had entered the compact kitchen and Whitney had paused with her back to him, so he took her shoulders and turned her around.

She looked up. "I see you perfectly."

"Good, because I want you to be able to judge how I feel and understand that I'm telling you the absolute truth."

"Why would I doubt you?"

This was it. The moment he had been dreading. "Because I'm about to confess something. It's important. Promise you'll hear me out?"

"What...?"

"Promise. First. Or I'll stop right now."

Her eyes widened. "All right. I promise. Please don't tell me you're an escaped convict. Or worse, that you're married."

"Neither."

"Whew! That's a relief."

With her gazing up at him, so beautiful, so trusting, the urge to hold and kiss her was strong. However, he knew better than to let anything sidetrack him.

"First, you have to stop looking at me that way," he warned.

"What way?" Her voice was pitched low, her lips slightly parted, palms resting gently on his chest.

"Good enough to kiss," he grumbled. "I'm trying to be serious here and you keep distracting me."

"I can hardly help that," she whispered, lowering her lashes. "I keep getting mixed signals."

"There's a reason," Josh told her. "I need to explain some things before I let myself get any more involved with you than I already am."

She dropped her hands and stepped back. "Sounds ominous."

"Not necessarily. It's about my income. I don't think it's fair to date you until we've talked that over."

"Is that all? Don't be silly!" A wide grin split her face. "I told you before that I don't care if you're struggling to make ends meet. I understand. You don't have to take me out on expensive dates to impress me. I'm a down-to-earth, country girl."

"That's not exactly what I meant." He reached for her hands and grasped them both while returning her grin.

"You don't have to make excuses, either," she insisted.

"You can see how I was raised. Both my parents worked. I know how hard it can be. I'm sure your mother has to watch her expenses, too, especially now that she's a widow."

"She does okay. I'm able to help her out when she needs it."

"Good. If you and I start seeing each other, that won't have to change. My job isn't anything to sneeze at. We can even go Dutch if that will make it easier on you."

Before Josh could reassure her further, Whitney added, "I told you I feel sorry for rich people. They always seem so unhappy and unfulfilled. I'd never want to live like that. Not in a million years."

"You have no desire to win the lottery?"

"Nope. Besides, I'd have to gamble to win and I never do, so I guess that's out."

"I guess so." He tried once more. "You could do a lot of good if you had plenty of money, you know. It's only bad if you give it the wrong importance in your life."

"I know. The Bible says it's the *love* of money that's the root of all evil, not money, itself. Still, I'm perfectly happy living here in Bygones and doing what I do. I'm so glad you feel the same."

He felt her squeeze his fingers as she mentioned his belonging. In another minute or two, when she'd heard all he had to say, would she be half as accepting?

Gripping her hands firmly so she couldn't pull away, he cleared his throat. "Whitney, listen carefully. My name is not Smith. It's Barton. Josh Barton. I founded Barton Technologies, the computer software company."

He waited.

She stared. Trembled.

Still, he kept hold of her, silently praying she would forgive his charade.

Her mouth had dropped open. Now she closed it. He could see the fire in her eyes, the stubborn set of her jaw.

Since she seemed struck speechless, he supplied the answers to her unspoken questions.

"Yes," Josh said softly, "I'm the one you've been calling Mr. Moneybags. The one who put Bygones back on its feet. Surely, you can't fault me for that."

"You—you *lied* to me. To all of us."

"If I had it to do over again, I'd tell the truth from the beginning," he insisted. "Remember, I wasn't a Christian when all this started. I thought I was doing the right thing then. Except for deceiving you, I still do."

She wrested her hands from his grasp and staggered backward until she bumped into the edge of the kitchen counter. "Everything has been one big lie."

"I honestly thought I was doing the right thing when I came here incognito. It was only later that I realized I'd made a mistake."

He began slowly shaking his head as he watched changing emotions flash across her face. Apparently, she was having trouble deciding if she hated him or wanted to thank him for bailing out her hometown.

Ultimately, he saw her make a decision.

She squared her shoulders, donned her discarded glasses and nodded. "All right. Let me go find my recorder and we can get started."

"What?"

"You heard me. Now that I know who Mr. Moneybags is, it's my duty to the *Gazette* to get the truth in print."

"You can't. Not yet."

"Why not? Do you think I owe you my silence when you've been playing me and this whole town for fools? Was it fun to laugh at us behind our backs, Josh?"

"It wasn't like that." He raised a hand as if taking an oath. "I swear it wasn't."

Whitney's eyes were sparking behind her glasses when she demanded, "Why should I believe you *this* time?"

"Because I'm telling you the truth."

"Hah! I doubt you know the meaning of the word."

His mind was scrambling for a way to diffuse her righteous anger. "Okay. Suppose I promise to announce everything, maybe at the theater, when I have lots of people all in one place? Will you wait that long?"

"No way. I have ethics, even if you don't. This is hot news and I'm going to write the story, one way or the other."

"You're mad at me."

Judging by the way she rolled her eyes and the face she made, she was a lot more than mad. She was rip-snorting infuriated. Reasoning with her when she was so upset was futile. What he needed to do was back off and give her time to think, to calm down and be reasonable.

Otherwise, he might as well abandon all his plans and leave Bygones immediately, because once it became common knowledge that he'd provided the finances for one project, he knew he'd be deluged with proposals for many others.

"All right," Josh said, forcing himself to act businesslike when what he wanted to do was pull her into his arms and kiss away her disappointment. "I'll give you a full interview. Tell you everything. All the details."

"Fine."

"After Christmas."

"Unacceptable."

"Then when? Where?" He studied her carefully. "You're way too wound up to do this tonight. We need to get together in some neutral place, perhaps with a disinterested third party to referee."

"And to chaperone," Whitney said, grimacing at him. "I cannot believe you took me in the way you did. Here I was, worried about you spending a lonely Christmas, and you could have thrown a party in any posh hotel in…where are you from?"

"St. Louis. I'm sure you'll do a computer search as soon as I leave and find out that much. Just remember, without the inside details that only I can provide, you won't have the scoop you need to win your Pulitzer."

The moment the gibe was out of his mouth he knew he'd made another terrible mistake. The expression of scorn Whitney sent his way was harsh enough to make his stomach churn.

Clearly, she was not the only one whose emotions were running high and out of control. In truth, he could see her actually winning such a coveted award some day, but bringing it up the way he had had made it sound as if he was taunting her.

"I'd better go," Josh said. "I'll let myself out."

Passing through the living room he bid her mother a polite good-night, grabbed his jacket and was out the door before anyone could react.

The way Whitney's thoughts were whirling, she likened them to the contents of the blender on the kitchen counter. Set on puree. It was embarrassing to have to admit she had been so thoroughly taken in, so completely fooled.

She *was* a fool, she reasoned. A fool for love. How could she have let herself fall for a guy whose past was unknown? The least she could have done was pursue her quest for answers more avidly.

"Only I didn't want to learn anything that might keep me from loving Josh," she muttered as tears slipped over her lashes and streamed down her cheeks.

She removed her glasses and grabbed a tissue, finally giving up, covering her face with both hands and sobbing.

A light touch on her shoulder and a sympathetic tone told her Betty had heard her weeping and had come to investigate.

"What is it, honey? Did he hurt you?"

"Not the way you're thinking," Whitney managed between sniffles and shaky breaths. "He's…he's…"

"He's what? Married?"

Whitney shook her head.

"Then what's the matter? Josh is a polite, mature person who obviously cares for you. If he's free, why are you crying?" Betty's voice hardened. "Did he tell you he wasn't interested in you? Because if he did, he's an idiot."

Pausing to blow her nose and struggling to control her emotions, Whitney kept shaking her head.

"Okay," her mother said. "I'll make us some hot cocoa and we can drink it while you pull yourself together. Chocolate always makes me feel better. How about you?"

Instead of answering her mother's question, Whitney took a fresh tissue and dabbed at her eyes. "His name isn't Smith," she whispered. "It's Barton."

The older woman looked puzzled. "So?"

"Barton, as in Barton Technologies."

"I still don't see…"

Whitney rolled her eyes and raised her shaky voice. "He's the one who donated all the money to help Bygones recover, Mom. He's rich."

"And that's a problem because…?

"Because he lied to me, to all of us. He came here under false pretenses and took everybody in with his simple-man act. He could probably buy and sell half of this town and never miss the money."

Betty's laugh made Whitney stare. "What's so funny?"

"You are. Think about what you just said. Josh Whatever-his-name-is has already bought half of downtown Bygones. And it's been the best thing to happen to this place in a lot of years."

"That's not the point."

"I think it is. The man was just trying to do good. How does that old saying go? 'No good deed goes unpunished'?"

"He didn't have to lie to all of us."

"No, he didn't. He could have stayed in his fancy office wherever he comes from and let someone else oversee his investments. Would that have pleased you?"

"It would have been better than lying."

"Okay. He made a mistake. The thing is, if he hadn't come to Bygones and made himself a part of this community he might never have joined a church and realized he'd been wrong. About a lot of things."

Lowering her voice, she put an arm around her daughter's shoulders and pulled her closer to add, "He never would have met you, either."

Whitney sniffled. "Right now, I wish I had never met *him*."

Chapter Fifteen

The first person Josh called after he got home that night was Coraline Connolly. When a deep voice answered her home phone he thought it might be Robert Randall until he heard a pleasant, "Mom! It's for you."

Coraline took the call in mere seconds. There was laughter in her voice. "Hello?"

"It's me. Josh," he said. "Sorry to bother you. It sounds like you have company."

"Just my son. That was Michael who answered. Chet and Cindy should be here by day after tomorrow."

"Then I shouldn't have called."

"Nonsense. You know I'm more than your SOS mentor. I'm your friend. If you need my help with something I'll be glad to give it."

"I hardly know where to start."

"You sound terrible, if you don't mind my saying so," Coraline observed. "What's wrong?"

"I took your advice."

"About what?"

"Whitney. I just told her who I was. She went ballistic."

"I see. Did you bother to mention that you were in love with her before you confessed?"

"That wouldn't have been fair to her."

"Nevertheless, it might have helped. What did you say?"

"I told her who I was and admitted to being the mysterious donor she's been trying to identify. I'd hoped she'd be thrilled, not tell me off for lying in the first place."

"How can I help you now?"

"By acting as our intermediary," Josh said. "She wants to interview me but she doesn't trust me anymore. I thought, if you were there, too, it might keep everybody calm and rational. What I've asked is that she hold off writing an exposé until I've had a chance to make an announcement to the entire town."

"That sounds reasonable. When were you planning to tell all?"

"Probably right after Christmas, when I screen the free movie in the theater. I thought that would work fine until Whitney started making noise about outing me immediately."

"How do you know she won't go ahead and do it anyway?"

"I don't. I promised her more details in the hope that would keep her from publishing until you and I'd had a chance to reason with her."

Coraline sighed audibly. "All right. When and where?"

"What do you suggest? I don't want to meet at her house and I don't think the coffee shop is appropriate."

"How about your upstairs apartment? Surely she won't balk if we tell her I'll be there, too."

"Do you think that's neutral enough ground?"

"Probably. And it will give you a chance to show her that you haven't been lording it over the rest of us. Actually, I can't believe how simply I've heard you've been living since you came to town."

Josh felt a glimmer of hope. "You really think that will help?"

"It can't hurt."

"I'm afraid she'd hang up on me if I phoned. Will you call her for me and set up our meeting?"

"For when?"

"Soon," Josh said. "How about Sunday night, after the evening service lets out?"

"Okay. Will you be there, too?"

"No. I plan to avoid Whitney at all costs until this is settled. I'm afraid seeing me will just make her madder."

"All right. And when I speak with her I'll also ask her to be patient. After all, she'll know everything by tomorrow night."

"I don't know how to thank you," Josh said with a sigh of relief.

Coraline laughed quietly. "If you really want to thank me, you might consider that idea I mentioned about opening a branch in Bygones."

"Blackmail?" Josh smiled at the phone.

"Let's just call it friendly persuasion," she replied.

"Actually, I've been giving your business suggestions serious thought and I can see a workable plan. I don't suppose Randall happens to be there with you?"

"As a matter of fact, he is. Do you want to speak with him about his empty factory building?"

"Yes, ma'am," Josh said, his smile broadening and his mood lifting. "No promises, but I guess it is time he and I had a talk."

In the background he heard her shout, "Robert! Robert! Josh wants to talk to you. Come quick!"

He was still chuckling when the other man came on the line and said, "Hello, Josh. Coraline tells me you've already invested plenty in Bygones. If you have any money left, how would you like to buy an industrial complex, too? I just happen to have one."

"I know you do," Josh admitted ruefully. "Actually, I've

already had my people look into it and check the specs for me."

Randall sounded pleased. "I'd heard you were smart. I'm happy to learn you're also sensible. I think you and I'll get along fine if you decide to do business with me."

"So do I," Josh said. "If and when I do put a new location into service, one of the things I'll need is a local consultant, somebody to help with hiring and overseeing operations. Are you fully retired or might you be interested in going back to work part-time?"

"You don't have to promise me a job to get a good deal on my property," Robert told him.

"I know I don't." Josh paused to give the other man a moment to think. "Just mull it over. All I ask is that you not make anything public until I've made up my mind whether or not to go ahead with it."

Randall sounded as if there was a frog in his throat when he said, "Either way, God bless you."

"He already has," Josh replied. "All I have to do now is keep from messing up His plans."

Whitney kept telling herself that the last person she wanted to accidentally encounter was Josh Smith, aka Barton. That didn't keep her from looking for him in church and everywhere else she went. Many men were wearing that same red hardware store cap, meaning that her pulse barely had time to slow before it got another jolt and resumed its wild galloping—until she realized that each person she was seeing was not Josh.

The more she tried to recall minute details of their last conversation, the less she was certain about. Had she really listened to him once he'd dropped the bombshell about being the town's secret benefactor? She was afraid she hadn't. And, in a way, she was sorry. Not sorry enough to change her opinion of his perfidy, of course. Just enough to be open to Coraline's call when it came.

"Of course I'll meet with you," Whitney said. "I think he made a wise choice when he asked you to sit in. I'll feel much more comfortable with you there."

"Good," the older woman said, "because we've decided to hold our little meeting in the private apartment above the Cozy Cup."

"Whoa. That's hardly what I'd call neutral territory."

"Actually, it is," Coraline insisted. "I think you need to see exactly how Josh has been living. Plus, he has a lot of equipment up there and wants to show you some of his work."

"What for?" Whitney's heart was threatening to beat its way out of her chest.

"If you intend to write an accurate article, surely you want to see what Barton Technologies does and how its CEO operates. He's been telecommuting to St. Louis rather than making trips home. His methods should be quite fascinating. That's what you're after, isn't it? The human interest details behind the overall project?"

"I guess so. When?"

"Very soon. My two youngest are arriving tomorrow and Michael is already home for the holidays. How about getting together this evening, right after services? Say around seven-thirty?"

Whitney nodded, then realized belatedly that Coraline couldn't see her motions. "Okay," she said haltingly. "I—I guess I can do that. Shall we rendezvous at the church?"

"Meaning, you don't want to take the chance you'll get to his shop before I do?"

"Exactly."

"Why don't you swing by my house and pick me up, instead? That way we'll be certain to arrive together and I won't have to leave my car out in the weather."

"Fine. I'll be there at a seven-thirty sharp."

As soon as the connection was broken, Whitney began to fret. She'd known she was going to have to face Josh sooner or later, and she did want her exclusive interview, of course. It was just the thought of looking into his sad eyes, of seeing a repetition of the disappointment she remembered from their last encounter, that put her off.

"I should not feel bad about a thing," she insisted, trying to convince the part of herself that kept questioning her motives. "I didn't lie to him. And I didn't pretend to be somebody I wasn't." *So why had Josh?*

Somewhere in the deep recess of her memory she seemed to recall a mention of his desire to do good. That was far from adequate justification. Neither was his lack of faith at the time he'd come to Bygones. Not being a Christian was no excuse to lie. He still should have told the whole truth up front.

What really galled her was how completely she'd been bamboozled. Some investigative reporter *she* was. Even if she did get the scoop she expected and manage to wow her editor with it, he was still bound to feel she had failed because it had taken her so long to root out the truth.

Which I didn't actually do, Whitney added, disgusted.

Josh had handed her the story himself, on a silver platter. All she had to do now was manage to push aside her personal anguish and actually listen to his explanation.

That was likely to be easier said than done.

Pacing his apartment, Josh kept an eye on the nearly deserted street and waited for his visitors. He'd straightened up the place even more than usual, hoping Whitney would like what she saw. As Coraline had wisely pointed out, he hadn't been living it up in secret. Yes, he liked some simple comforts but he had not invested lavishly in the small quarters above his shop. All he'd really craved was a quiet, secluded place to work. Beyond that, his needs were minimal.

The sight of Whitney's rag-top Mustang parking below made his pulse race. He hurried down the stairs, ready to welcome her.

When he reached the glass door, however, he saw two people waiting on the sidewalk. Coraline and Whitney had ridden together.

Smiling through his trepidation, he unlocked the door and swung it open. "Come in. Can I fix either of you something to drink? Coffee? Cocoa?"

"Nothing for me, thanks," the gray-haired woman said pleasantly. Whitney merely shook her head and wiped her feet on the mat.

"Okay. Follow me."

As he led the way back upstairs, Josh could feel Whitney watching him. It was as if he was so in tune with everything about her, her gaze was palpable.

He'd left the door to his apartment ajar. Now, he gave it a nudge and it swung open. "Ladies first."

Coraline entered, followed closely by the young woman whose mere glance set him on edge and made his heart do funny things, not to mention muddling his usually clear thinking.

"It's not very cozy," Coraline remarked. "Actually, except for the carpet and kitchenette, it looks more like a lab than a home."

"That's pretty much all it is," Josh replied. "I saw no reason to decorate or add more furniture than I needed."

He pulled out the padded desk chair for her, then added a side chair from his kitchen area for Whitney. "Please, have a seat."

Although she perched on the edge of the wooden chair, he thought Whitney was starting to relax. At least he hoped she was.

There was only one other chair available, the second one from his kitchen, so he brought it forward and swung a leg over the seat, occupying it backwards so he could lean his arms across the back.

"Sorry about the hard chairs. I don't normally have visitors."

Whitney was scanning the sparsely furnished quarters. "This is it? You bought a whole city block and this is the best you could do for yourself?"

Josh snorted derisively. "I could have made it into a lush penthouse, I suppose. I just saw no need. This is good enough for my purposes."

He watched her take her recorder, pen and paper out of her familiar tote. "Let's start with the past. What brought you to Bygones in the first place? Why here? Why us?"

"Didn't Coraline tell you? My mother was born and raised here."

Whitney's eyes narrowed and snapped to her companion. "She hasn't told me much of anything."

"That's because I made her promise not to," he said, directing his explanation to the reporter. "She hasn't known the truth for very long. It was my resemblance to my mother, Susanna Hastings, that finally tipped her off. Mom used to go to school here in Bygones before she went off to college in St. Louis. That's where she met and married my dad, Bruce Barton. She never came back here again."

"Why didn't she visit? It isn't that far. How long is the drive? About four hours?"

"In good weather." Josh took a deep, settling breath and nodded. "Her parents were deceased and I've already told you a little about my father. You'd have to have known him personally to truly understand. Every time Mom would start to reminisce, he'd lecture her about never being able to recapture the past. It wasn't until Ms. Coraline sent out reunion invitations, then had to cancel the event due to a lack of community funds, that I started to think about how I might be able to help."

"Why didn't you just fund the reunion?" Whitney asked.

He shrugged. "That would have been like putting a little piece of adhesive tape on a broken arm. Once I decided to help this town recover, I could see it needed more than a temporary influx of cash. It needed to rediscover itself and grow."

When Whitney didn't comment, Josh looked to Coraline for moral support. "My original plan was to simply work through Ms. Coraline and my lawyers, but then I decided it would be even better if nobody knew where the money was coming from."

"Were you worried about being cheated?"

"At first I may have been, I guess." He raked his fingers through his hair before folding his arms across the back of the chair again. "I thought, if I became one of the new shopkeepers, I could keep an eye on the whole operation without making anybody nervous."

"Why should they be nervous?"

"Unexpected windfalls affect people's opinions," Josh explained. "They may think they're staying neutral but they don't. They can't. They're always either looking to see if the donor is watching them or keeping an eye out to try to figure out what's coming next. There is absolutely no way to become a true part of a community when people know who you really are. I know. I've tried before."

Coraline had remained silent until now. "He's right," she said. "Think about it. Put yourself in Josh's place."

"I don't see how that would help," Whitney argued.

"Suppose he had shown up here in rags. Would you and the Community Church congregation have taken him in, clothed and fed him, the way Jesus says to?"

"Of course we would." Whitney sounded indignant.

"Then why reject him for another reason?"

"That's not what's happening here."

Speaking softly, gently, Josh said, "In that case, tell me you forgive me."

Whitney clicked off the recorder and began blinking rapidly. Off to one side, the school principal reached into her handbag and produced a fistful of tissues which she passed to Whitney without comment.

Dabbing at her eyes, Whitney rose and slipped the recorder back into her tote.

Coraline wisely stood, as well. "Perhaps we should finish this chat another time," she told Josh. "I really need to get back to my family. Michael will be expecting me."

Josh opened the apartment door and escorted the women downstairs so he could unlock the shop to let them out.

Whitney had not even glanced his way since she'd begun to cry. He hated to just let her walk away when she obviously needed comforting.

As they approached the heavy glass door he paused and started to reach toward her.

Coraline caught his eye and shook her head, mouthing, "No."

Letting Whitney go at that moment was almost more than Josh could manage. Nevertheless, he nodded and stepped aside.

Once the women reached the Mustang, he was relieved to see Whitney hand her keys over so Coraline could drive.

Good. At least he wouldn't have to worry about her getting in a wreck because tears were messing up her vision. Still, he was apprehensive about letting them leave when so little had actually been settled.

They would probably drive to the principal's first, he reasoned. That should be safe enough. Later, however, Whitney would try to go home by herself, and if she continued to be so upset, there was no telling how well she'd cope. Or how competently she'd handle the car.

There was only one thing Josh could do and still live with himself. He'd have to follow her and make sure she was all right.

Nothing short of seeing to her well-being in person would suffice.

It didn't matter that she had failed to forgive him or that she was weeping because he'd made a terrible mistake.

He still loved her with all his heart.

Something told him he always would.

Chapter Sixteen

By the time Coraline stopped the car and put it in park so they could change drivers, Whitney had managed to regain control of herself. She desperately hoped she was calm enough to convince her companion to let her leave.

"Are you sure you don't want to come in and say hello to Michael?" Coraline asked, obviously concerned.

"Not now. My eyes are red and puffy. My sinuses are killing me, too, thanks to this icy weather."

"All right." The principal leaned in to pat Whitney's arm before straightening and preparing to close the driver's door for her. "I suppose it would be best if you waited. I want you to present your best self. It's been years since my Michael has seen you and he is still single, you know."

Matchmaking? Now? Whitney gritted her teeth to keep from saying something she might regret. Why was life so complicated? And why did everybody seem to think she couldn't be happy if she was unmarried?

Probably because I don't exactly look overjoyed at the moment, Whitney answered silently. Nothing in her life made sense anymore. Not when all she could think about was Josh Sm… Barton.

"I'll be fine, Ms. Coraline. You'd better get inside before you take a chill."

"Drive safely." Straightening, she stepped back and waved a gloved hand.

Whitney waited, headlights illuminating the path to the front porch, until her friend had made it safely to the door and gone inside. Then, she continued to sit very still for long seconds before finally backing out and driving away.

Fleeing from the churning thoughts that raced and tumbled through her mind like a Kansas tornado, she decided to take the long way home. Anything was better than facing an immediate barrage of parental questions. There was nothing like a weeping daughter to bring out a mother's protective instincts.

Whitney had no idea how to rationalize her tears, even to herself. Josh's confession had battered her ego. Made her question her skills as well as her opinions. Could Coraline have been right? Was she treating him like a pariah when she should be receiving his admission of well-meaning duplicity with grace and forgiveness?

No matter how often Whitney denied her own guilt or how many times she insisted that the fault was all Josh's, her conscience knew better. The man had asked for forgiveness and she had given him self-righteous anger, instead. What kind of Christian would refuse to heed a heartfelt story of repentance?

Once again, her eyes filled with tears, misting her vision and making the glow from the streetlights seem to flicker. To help distract herself she turned on the car's CD player to listen to beautiful, uplifting, Christmas music. That helped, but not enough to make her forget the hurt look on Josh's face or the way his eyes had seemed to plead for understanding.

New snow was beginning to fall faster. Whitney slowed her car and increased the speed of her windshield wipers. Their path was marked by arcs of icy residue, the view further distorted by condensation on the inside of the glass.

She leaned forward to swipe away the moisture, peering out at the rapidly disappearing ruts in the slush, and belatedly wishing she had chosen a more direct route home.

An approaching vehicle's headlights blinded her for a moment. Unsure of the roadway edges, she took her foot all the way off the gas.

The other car passed, leaving swirling snowflakes in its wake that erased everything.

Whitney stepped on the brake. At least that was her intent.

Instead of slowing, however, her car suddenly accelerated!

That was *wrong.* She wanted to stop, not go faster.

Reacting on pure instinct, she pushed harder on the pedal.

The yellow Mustang sprang ahead like its namesake being spurred by a wild cowboy.

Whitney screamed.

Tires on one side of the car ran up onto a snow bank that had been left when the road was plowed. The vehicle slid and tilted precariously.

Hands fisted on the wheel, teeth gritted, she hung on and turned into the skid, just as she'd been taught.

This time, however, with half her wheels already off the road and the others lacking proper traction, the maneuver failed to right her.

All she had time for was a high-pitched, "God! Help!" before her car circled to face the way she'd come and tipped past its center of gravity.

Held fast by her seat belt, Whitney hung on tight and ducked.

The metal ribs holding the canvas top collapsed above her.

Grinding, rending sounds stopped almost immediately. The yellow car teetered on its side, its top resting against the piled snow, the driver's door at the bottom. If not for her seat belt, she might have been thrown out and crushed.

Silence enveloped Whitney. So did frigid snow.

Trapped by the car's seat on one side and the collapsed top on the other, all Whitney could do was try to catch her breath and pray.

Neither was easy.

According to Coraline, Josh had just missed catching Whitney. He wouldn't have thought much about it except he had failed to pass her on the road.

He backed the van into the street and peered through the curtain of snowflakes. This was a wet snow. It stuck to everything it touched, clumping and building up in front of his windshield wipers until they squealed against the icy glass.

The streets were deserted. Citizens of Bygones had retired for the night, sensibly waiting out the storm in the comfort of their homes.

"All except Whitney," he murmured. "Where did you go?"

The urge to pray for guidance hit him. But what should he ask for? What good would it do to agonize over the situation when he could be taking action, instead? His life had been stable, predictable, *normal* until that obsessive reporter had entered it. Now, nothing made sense the way it once had.

Josh snorted in self-derision. Talk about obsessive. He was worse than Whitney when it came to their relationship. *Assuming there is one,* he added in disgust.

He inched away from Coraline's house and headed for Granary Road, hardly thinking, barely conscious of his course.

The inability to see things clearly was not merely one of his current physical world, he realized with astonishment. It was a problem in the spiritual realm, too. He had assumed, because he had begun his life in Bygones with a misleading identity and had not meant to hurt anyone, he hadn't done anything really wrong.

Now that he was able to step back and assess his actions from Whitney's point of view, he had to rethink that conclusion. In her place, he might have been just as upset.

Sighing, he finally succumbed to the urge to pray. "I'm not good at this, Father," he began. "I don't sound like all those guys who lead prayers in church and I may not even be doing this right. Cut me some slack, okay? I never meant to hurt anybody, especially not Whitney. Help me find her? Please? I just need to see that she's all right. Then I'll leave her alone if that's what she really wants."

Josh tightened his jaw, his hands gripping the steering wheel, his heart pounding as if he'd just run a marathon. What else was he supposed to say? Oh, yeah. "In Jesus's name. Amen."

He'd had so little experience with answered prayer he wondered if he'd recognize God's leading if and when he got it. He sure hoped so. Because this was a horrible night for anybody to be caught outside in the cold, not to mention trying to drive on such slick roadways.

He came to an intersection and decided to detour past Whitney's house and see if he could tell whether or not her car was in the garage. If it wasn't, he was just going to have to break down and call her on her cell. There was no way he was going to go back to his apartment until he knew for sure that she was okay.

The Mustang's motor had died when she'd rolled her poor car over. To be on the safe side, Whitney turned off the key, as well.

Given the configuration of the wreck, she figured that the passenger door had to be unencumbered. Her problem was that the seat belt held her where she lay and its buckle was trapped beneath her.

Trying to reach around and release the catch she discovered that her left arm was too short. The right one was pinned beneath her and generally useless unless she could somehow work it free. Therefore, she was trapped.

That wouldn't have been too bad if she had been closer to downtown where someone would find her in a reasonable amount of time. Unfortunately, she was not. Nor was she positive exactly where she had been when she'd lost control. Too bad she'd failed to add a GPS unit to her old car.

Cold was seeping into the wreck. Whitney shivered, wondering if it was just as well she could not feel her feet. She tried to wiggle her toes and thought she succeeded, mainly because a hundred tiny needles pricked at them and pain shot up her legs.

Her hands and arms were getting numb, too. Where the snow had come in contact with warmth it had melted, wetting her clothing before starting to return to its frozen state.

Fuzzy thinking kept her from true prayer, although she did silently call out to her heavenly Father. She wanted to weep, for herself and for the people who cared about her and would grieve if she wasn't found before it was too late.

"Is this how it ends?" she whispered. "Am I going to die?"

Seeking comfort from her faith, she once again reached for the key, only this time she turned it to accessory so she could drift off listening to carols. If these were her final few minutes of consciousness she wanted to hear praises and feel God's presence.

The music on the CD sounded louder in the enclosed, otherwise silent space but she didn't try to lower the volume. Instead, she let the melodies carry her spirit higher and higher, until she finally closed her eyes and drifted off.

* * *

Amid the flurries, Josh had apparently missed the turn that would have taken him directly to Whitney's house. He muttered to himself, angry that a mere storm had kept him from his goal.

"Now what?" he grumbled, banging his fists against the steering wheel. "Where am I? Which way?"

If this was God's idea of an answer to prayer he might have to rethink his belief system, that was for sure.

It occurred to him that wandering around in a blizzard was about the dumbest stunt he'd ever pulled, never mind his reasons. What he ought to do was try to figure out which way was home and turn around right now.

But he wouldn't. He couldn't. Not unless he was certain Whitney was safe and sound.

The way Josh saw it, he had several reasonably intelligent choices. He could call her cell. Even if she hung up on him at least he'd quit worrying. Or, he could dial her house phone, but if she hadn't made it home that would worry her parents unnecessarily.

The cell was by far the best option. Stopping at the side of the road near an intersection, he left the motor running and pulled out his cellular phone. It was state of the art, of course, since he always kept up with the latest trends.

Astounded that he'd been too rattled to think clearly, he stared at the screen, realizing he had a navigation app. He might not know where he was but his phone did!

That left only Whitney to worry about.

He found her private number in the phone's memory and keyed it. The screen immediately displayed a "failure to connect" message.

That made no sense, since he had a strong signal. Perhaps the snow and ice were interfering with one of the cell towers that relayed calls.

Zipping his jacket, he turned up his collar, opened the van door and stepped out into the falling snow to try again.

The result was the same. No connection. No reception.

Frustrated and growing more and more concerned about the woman who had stolen his heart, he started to climb back into the van.

Wherever he was, somebody in the distance was broadcasting Christmas music just like the merchants played over loudspeakers to get their customers in the mood to shop.

Josh gritted his teeth. The last thing he wanted to think about right now was a holiday, happy or otherwise. All he cared about was finding Whitney.

And when he did, he was going to take her in His arms and kiss her silly, even if she slapped his face. She was going to listen to him. She had to. There was no way he could just step back and let their love waste away.

Yes, he told himself. *I love her.* No more questions remained, at least not in his mind. If she still refused to forgive him after he confessed his love, then he'd find a way to accept that.

But if, as he hoped, her tears had meant that she was softening toward him, he wanted to hear that from her, face to face.

His telltale lopsided smile lifted one corner of his mouth as he slid behind the wheel again. Now that he had made up his mind to confront her again, as soon as possible, he was feeling much better.

That relief was short-lived, however. The minute he stepped on the gas, intending to pull back onto the roadway, his rear wheels began to slip.

Josh gunned the motor. The tires churned up slushy snow, then spun wildly.

He gave up trying to accelerate, got out and circled the van, peering at the ground where his efforts had left deep ruts.

There was no getting around it. The van was buried up

to its rear axle. He wasn't going anywhere. At least not without help.

Checking his location again via the phone app, he looked up the number for the closest garage, which happened to be Dill's place, and called to request a tow truck.

Then he climbed back into the van, slammed the door and rubbed his freezing hands together to warm them.

Hopefully, he wasn't going to have to wait too long.

Chapter Seventeen

The frosty air inside the toppled car was either getting warmer or Whitney's breath was shallow and cooling, because it no longer made such noticeable clouds in front of her face when she exhaled.

Shivering constantly, she kept dozing off, sometimes feeling as if the Lord was cradling her in his arms and other times sensing the tangible danger of her situation.

"Surely someone will miss me and come looking soon," she muttered. *But who?* Coraline thought she'd gone straight home, her parents would assume she was still working on her interview, and Josh was probably doing his best to forget they'd ever met.

By turning her head, Whitney could see the unbroken side window that was now above her. When she'd first had the accident and ended up like this, she'd been able to detect the glow from a nearby streetlamp. Now, the entire window was blanketed with freshly fallen snow, blotting out most of the light.

Huddling in darkness, growing weaker and weaker as the icy night crept into her very bones, she closed her eyes.

"Am I done, Father?" she prayed. "Is this the end of my struggles? I hope not, because there are a lot of things I've left unfinished. A lot of people who need to hear me say

I love them. And not only Josh. I love my parents and my friends, and practically everyone in Bygones."

Whitney sniffled, wondering if she was hallucinating when she thought she heard a motor.

She stopped the CD music. Held her breath. Listened. Prayed without further words.

The engine roar built until it was nearly on top of her. Then, to her shock and dismay, it passed by!

How could anyone have come that close without noticing her car? Was it so buried in fresh snow that it was invisible? How was that possible? How long had she been lying there?

Panic rose and took control. She began to struggle against the seat belt that was meant to protect her and was, instead, trapping her in the car where she was in real danger of dying from hypothermia.

"Hey! Over here," she screeched. "Help! Help me!"

The roar was fading. So were her chances of survival.

Josh hopped out as soon as the headlights of the wrecker bathed his van.

"Glad you found me," he told the driver, recognizing the bundled up Elwood Dill mostly by his beard.

"I should be home keepin' warm like a sensible person," Elwood said. "We both should."

Josh shook his hand. "Yeah, well. Thanks for coming so fast. It's getting really cold and I didn't think it was smart to run the heater when the exhaust pipe was filled with snow."

"Depends on how cold you got," the aging hippie said amiably as he pulled on heavy gloves. "You're lucky I didn't make the mistake of stopping at that other wreck."

Josh was already on edge. When Elwood mentioned an accident, his instincts insisted he learn all the details. "What wreck? Where?"

"I passed it a quarter of a mile or so east of here, on the

other side of the park. The car looks like it's been there for a while. Probably crashed hours ago."

"What car? What did it look like?" Josh almost grabbed the man's thin shoulders through his padded, canvas jacket and shook him.

"Like a dead turtle," Elwood said with a grin. "Some guy flipped over and landed sideways in a snow bank. Probably hitched a ride home and left the car. I'll call the police and see if Chief Sheridan wants to send somebody out to check on it. You know Joe, don't you?"

"Yeah, yeah. Tell me more about the car. What color was it?"

"Beats me. There was a lot of snow covering it. All I saw was the undercarriage and a couple of tires stickin' up." He bent down to start hitching a chain to the towing hooks behind the front bumper of Josh's van.

"Leave that," Josh shouted, grabbing his arm and hauling him bodily back toward his truck. "Show me that other car."

"Hey, man, I got dispatched to help you," the other man said, twisting free. "If I go off on my own like you want, Velma'll have a cow."

"Then sell me your truck," Josh demanded, reaching for his wallet. "How much?"

"Whoa. Hold on, son. You can't afford to buy my wrecker, even if it is old. Now calm down and let's get you pulled out of that ditch."

Josh had always relied upon his wits to get what he wanted. Now, he was beginning to wonder if a more direct approach was warranted. He thought about trying to make off with the tow truck, but figured that wouldn't be smart because he didn't know exactly where Elwood had seen the wrecked car. Even if it wasn't Whitney's, someone else could be in trouble.

Rational thought provided the answer. He redialed the last number he'd called. A woman answered. "Velma?"

"Speaking."

"This is Josh Smith, again," he said. "Your husband is here but I need him to take care of another car before mine. Do you have any problem with that? I'll pay for both calls."

"It's okay with me," she said.

"Great. Thanks. Now tell Elwood yourself, will you, so he knows it's okay to divert." Josh handed over the phone.

"Okay, okay, hon," Dill said, frowning, "but if you don't hear from me in a few minutes, send the cops out here. The coffee guy is actin' real crazy."

Josh grabbed his phone out of the man's hand and headed for the truck at a run. "Come on. Let's go."

"I can't just leave my chain in the street. It'll only take a minute to gather it up."

"A hundred-dollar bonus if you come now!" Josh shouted.

"Well…"

"Five hundred. Cash!"

"Since you put it that way." Elwood began to saunter back toward the wrecker.

Josh leaned out the half-open passenger door and yelled, "A thousand if you run."

The incredulous driver was still grinning and shaking his head as he climbed behind the wheel and started the enormous truck.

His smile faded and his jaw dropped when Josh shoved a handful of crisp, hundred dollar bills into his nearest hand and roared, "Drive!"

There was that engine sound again! Whitney was so cold, so slow to react, she wasn't sure she could muster enough energy or focus well enough to call for help.

She gasped in as much frigid air as she could stand and tried to shout. The feeble cry sounded as if it was coming from someone else. Someone far, far away.

"Help," she tried again, this time able to put more force behind her shout. "Help me!"

To her relief, the vehicle didn't roar past. It stopped. Idled.

She blinked, staring up at the side window that was now her roof. Was that movement? *Yes!*

The layer of fluffy snow was being brushed off. A bright light shone through and made her eyes water.

Someone was shouting. Calling her name. She'd been saved!

Tears flowed freely, streaking her face and wetting one cheek as gravity pulled them downward.

She heard a man yell, "She's alive!"

All she could think at that moment was, "Praise the Lord, I'm getting a second chance."

"We need to break this window," Josh told the wrecker owner.

"That'll drop glass all over her. Let's get the fire department and do this right."

"We can't just leave her there. Look at her. She's blue already."

"But she's moving. That's a good sign."

"Good enough for you, maybe, but not for me." Josh took a firm hold on the only visible door handle and tried to budge it. The Mustang wobbled but stayed on its side.

"Here. Help me. Maybe we can get it back on all four tires."

Elwood shook his head and raised both hands. "Best not move her. If she was hurt in the crash we could do more harm than good."

Josh knew all that. He was an educated man. The problem was that his intellect had taken a backseat to his emotions and he wasn't ready to relinquish control to his more sensible side.

When the truck driver jogged back to his rig and used his radio to call for police and fire assistance, Josh cupped his hands around his eyes to help him see and peered through the passenger side window again.

Whitney was no longer stirring. Her head had dropped onto her shoulder. He couldn't be sure of her condition because her scarf had fallen against her cheek and was hiding most of her face.

His heart immediately clenched. "Whitney! Honey, look at me. It's Josh. Whitney?"

She didn't move. Didn't even twitch. Either she had passed out or was asleep or…

The notion of losing her after everything he'd done to find her and tell her how he felt, was unacceptable.

His fist slammed into the window, over and over. It didn't even crack.

Looking around for something, anything, hard and sharp, he came up empty. Hands in his pockets, he wondered if hitting the glass with his phone would work. Then his fist closed on his key ring. "Maybe."

He held them tight with several bunched together and sticking out like a knife. The first blow didn't work. Neither did the second.

"Whitney!" he cried, his voice filled with pathos and agony. "Whitney. Wake up!"

She didn't move.

Behind him, Josh sensed Dill's return. The man had brought a tire iron from the truck.

"You don't have to hit it hard," Elwood cautioned. "Safety glass breaks pretty easy if you use the right tool. The pieces should be small and kinda square. Just tell her to cover her eyes."

"They're covered," Josh replied, so breathless he could barely function. "Here goes."

* * *

The tinkling Whitney was hearing reminded her of tiny silver Christmas bells, perhaps like the ones Lily had fastened to each of the door wreaths she'd made for Main Street merchants.

Her thoughts drifted, then began to coalesce, as thin as ether, yet as intense as love could make them.

"Josh," she whispered, imagining the impossible, thinking he was there beside her.

A gentle hand cupped her cheek and supported her head. She nestled into the palm, content with her fantasy. The cold began to fade. Warm, minty breath tickled her senses. She fought to open her eyes.

"Whitney?"

What a lovely dream, she thought. *Josh is here. Josh is...*

Her lashes fluttered. She opened her eyes ever so slightly. There *was* a physically powerful presence there with her. If this was a figment of her imagination, it sure looked a lot like her favorite barista.

"Josh?"

"Hold perfectly still, honey. The fire department is on its way."

She began to struggle. To regain her senses. To revert to her usual self. "I'm fine. Really. I just—can't—get—this—stupid—seat—belt—undone."

"You're sure nothing is broken? The cold might have numbed an injury."

"I wasn't this cold when I first landed," Whitney insisted. The urge to sink back into unconsciousness was strong. She fought it with her last ounces of strength and won. "I had plenty of time to take inventory."

"All right." He gently released her head and backed away. That was when Whitney saw he'd been hanging above her, half in and half out of the car.

In the distance she heard sirens that grew louder by the

second. The rescue squad was coming. That was nice, but she wanted someone else much more.

"Josh! Don't leave me." It wasn't a loud cry but it had the hoped-for result.

He stuck his head and shoulders back through the broken window. "I'm still here. Hang tight, Whitney. They'll have you out in no time."

Relief, coupled with more joy than she'd ever felt before, were enough to renew a portion of her normal sense of humor.

Shivering all over she nevertheless made a silly face at him. "Did you really just tell me to *hang tight?*"

"I didn't mean…"

By this time Whitney was starting to chuckle. "Never mind," she said, laughing quietly. "We'll talk about saying what we mean and meaning what we say after they get me out of this car."

Extrication took far longer than Josh wanted. Yes, he understood the need for care and for stabilizing her, just in case, but a pot of steaming coffee would have frozen solid by the time they finally lifted the love of his life from her mashed car and strapped her to a backboard.

An ambulance was waiting. Josh took Whitney's hand and walked next to her as the attendants carried her to it.

"I told you, I'm fine," she insisted. "Just cold, that's all. I was wearing my seat belt, as you well know."

"Let them check you out, honey," Josh said. "I'll stay right with you. I promise."

He watched her icy lashes dampen with unshed tears. "How did you find me? How did anybody find me?"

For the first time since he'd mired his van in the slush, it occurred to Josh that he'd received the answer to his prayers, only not in the manner he'd envisioned.

"It's a really long story," he said, brushing bits of safety glass from her hair.

The attendants loaded her onto a gurney and slid it into the back of the ambulance. One of them tried to stop Josh from boarding. He resisted.

"You'd better let him ride with her or next thing you know he'll be trying to buy your ambulance," Elwood called out. "He thinks he's Santa Claus or something."

"Or something," Whitney said quietly, reaching for his hand and holding tight as her tears finally slid past her temples to wet the white sheet beneath her. "I have a lot of apologizing to do." She sniffled when she saw hurt in his eyes. "I'm so sorry, Josh."

"So am I, honey. All I wanted was to do a good deed."

"I believe you. Your heart was always in the right place. It's mine that was confused."

I'm not confused anymore, though, she realized. The sight of Josh when she'd opened her eyes inside that frigid death trap had been the answer to more than her current prayers. Unless she was imagining things, and she didn't think she was, he was the answer to those divine pleas that had come before—and those in the future.

The big story was no longer dependent upon the identity of Mr. Moneybags. The truly important information was warming her heart and making her soul sing praises to the Lord.

She was alive! And the man she loved was not only beside her, holding her hand, he had been the instrument of her rescue. God had used him to find her, to save her life. Anyone could have done it, yet in His wisdom, their heavenly Father had chosen to send Josh. To cement their shaky relationship with the glue of circumstances that had brought out the best in both of them and had demonstrated a love that could not be denied.

Closing her eyes as the ambulance headed for the highway that would take them to the emergency room in Manhattan, she clasped his hand and praised the Lord until fatigue and the swaying movement of the vehicle finally lulled her to sleep.

Chapter Eighteen

"There's nothing like a few hours of sleep to give a girl back her energy," Whitney said as Josh drove them back to Bygones.

He was so happy to have her out of the hospital and close beside him in the rental car, he couldn't stop grinning. "Try thirty-seven hours."

"It couldn't have been that long. You're exaggerating."

"Okay. What day is this?"

"Um, Monday?"

"Tuesday."

"It's Christmas Eve? Already?"

"Sure is. I hope you have all your shopping done because like it or not, Christmas is almost here."

"Oh, dear."

He reached over and clasped her hand. "Hey, don't sweat the small stuff. You can find just about any gift you need in Bygones."

"Thanks to your generosity, I can," Whitney said. The warmth of her gaze made him happier than he could ever remember being, even as a little boy. There was something about this town and its people that had gotten under his skin and made him realize what he'd been missing. No wonder his mother missed the place so much. And speaking of parents…

Josh cleared his throat. “I’m going to drop you at home like I promised your folks, then have Elwood return this rental car for me.”

“Okay.” The way she drew out her reply told him that she’d surmised more than he’d just told her.

“I need to go back to St. Louis for a few days and take care of some business in person.” He gave her fingers a tender squeeze. “I won’t be gone long.”

“Do you have to go right now? It’s almost Christmas.”

“I know. And I’m sorry about that. I’ll phone and let you know how things are progressing.”

“Things? What things?”

“Who wants to know? Are you back to being a reporter again so soon?”

“You did promise to give me a scoop so I could tell all in the next issue of the *Gazette.* We’ll publish a couple of days late this week to avoid having to work on Christmas Eve or Christmas Day. It’ll be a weekend extra.”

“That should be perfect,” Josh said, elated yet trying not to show too much excitement before he had everything finalized. “I’ll give you more details as soon as you’re ready to work again.”

“I’m ready now,” Whitney insisted.

He laughed tenderly and cast her a loving glance. “I have no doubt. But don’t you think it would be best if you had your recorder and laptop at hand before I started citing details?”

“My laptop! It was in the car when I wrecked. It’s probably ruined.”

“Nope. I had your mother bring it to me when she visited you in the hospital so I could check it out. All your personal belongings have been rescued and are waiting for you at home—in perfect working order.”

"You think of everything."

"I try." He sobered. "Which brings me to my upcoming trip. There are some decisions that require me to be in the office for face-to-face negotiations. I hate to leave you when you've just gotten back on your feet but it can't be helped. Please don't be upset."

"How could I be mad at a guy who not only saved my life but saved my whole hometown?"

"I was hoping you'd see it that way." Josh was shaking his head as he pondered the events that had brought them together. "As amazing as it seems, I believe God had His hand in the whole process, start to finish. Of course, I didn't know it at first, but looking back I can sure see that possibility."

"Even your getting the van stuck and calling Elwood," Whitney added. "I was talking to Mom about that after I woke up in the hospital."

"She agrees?"

"Absolutely. Plus, she has a theory about other elements of your role in all our lives."

"I'm looking forward to hearing it." He brought the rented sedan to a smooth stop in the Leigh driveway. "Do you want me to walk you in?"

He saw disappointment in Whitney's countenance before she unsnapped the seat belt and yanked on the door handle. "Are you in *that* much of a hurry?"

"Sorry. I'm afraid I am."

"Then go. I can manage."

He wanted to tell her he loved her, the way he had when she'd been sound asleep in her hospital room in Manhattan. Now just wasn't the right time or place. Whitney was an intricate part of his elaborate plans; plans he had finalized in his mind while sitting by her bedside and thanking the Lord that she had survived. It would all come together soon.

And, in the meantime, he had a million details that needed his personal touch, particularly since the upcoming holidays would keep many workers at home.

Josh waved as he watched her make her way to the door where Betty waited with open arms.

Whitney's mother returned his wave, then nudged her daughter.

Josh almost piled out of the car and ran to Whitney when she turned and he thought he saw unshed tears sparkling in her emerald eyes.

She raised her hand and waved goodbye, looking as if her best friend was about to depart.

That thought settled in his heart and mind, warming him all the way to his core. He would like nothing better than to be her best friend—and husband—for the rest of her life.

Now, all he had to do was convince her.

Whitney let Betty shepherd her into the house. "I can't believe Josh is leaving, just like that."

"You had plenty of privacy on the drive home from Manhattan. Didn't you talk at all?"

"Of course we did. He insisted he had to take care of some important business that couldn't wait."

"Well then?"

"Well, why couldn't he delegate? There has to be someone else who's been minding his interests while he played barista here in Bygones. Why can't he let them handle his affairs for another week or so?"

"I don't know, dear. Did you ask him?"

Whitney pouted and shook her head. "No."

"Why not? I thought, after your accident and all those hours in the hospital, you and he were a couple."

"You did?"

"Of course. Don't you remember anything? Josh stayed

with you day and night. I had trouble even convincing him to take a break to eat."

"He did say I'd been out of it for days. I can't believe it's almost Christmas." She smiled for her mother's sake and admired the tree she and Josh had decorated. "That did turn out pretty, didn't it?"

"Yes, it did. Dad didn't want me to fuss with anything this year. When you bought that tree for us, I was delighted."

"Can I make a confession?" Whitney asked, blushing.

"If you're going to tell me you did it in order to get Josh involved in the holidays and spend more time with him, never mind. We'd already figured that out." She laughed softly and gave her daughter's shoulders a hug.

Whitney winced.

"Sorry. Did I hurt you? I thought your seat belt had kept you from injury. That's what the doctors said."

"I'm kind of bruised," Whitney admitted. "The belt did keep me from flying out of the car when it rolled but it left me pretty sore where it held me so tightly."

"Did you tell Josh? I doubt he'd have left so quickly if he'd known you were still hurting."

"I didn't see any reason to mention it. He kept going on and on about having to head for St. Louis and being behind in his work, so I kept my mouth shut."

Betty eyebrows arched in an unspoken question.

"Okay," Whitney said with a grin. "Maybe my mouth wasn't exactly shut. I just didn't ask for sympathy."

"But you did tell him how you feel about him, didn't you?"

Whitney shook her head. "I was going to. I thought we'd get home and he could come in and…"

"And he left, instead."

She nodded and grimaced. "He sure did. Like somebody had lit a fire under him and he couldn't wait to hit the road."

True to his word, Josh phoned Whitney that same evening. "Hi. How are you feeling?"

"Fine."

He did not like the controlled tone of her voice. "Are you sure?"

"Positive. Are you calling to finish giving me details for my exclusive story? I'm ready."

"All right." Sighing, he began to tell her more about his mother's longtime friendship with Coraline Connolly and his reasons for starting the Save Our Streets restoration project after he'd learned that Bygones was dying.

"What about the shopkeepers and their businesses? How did you choose them?"

"I had my attorneys draw up a set of qualifications and we went from there."

"Miss Coraline really had no idea?"

"Not until recently. I told you that."

"Just trying to get everything straight. How did you manage to be chosen over all those other applicants? I mean, if the process was fair, how did you end up as a winner?"

"The final say was through the dummy corporation that was funneling the money. Since I was their sole member, it was easy."

"What about now? Are you going to stop helping now that your role in the town's revival is going to be made public?"

Josh was glad she couldn't see his expression because he was frowning. "Of *course* not."

"But you are planning to leave Bygones, aren't you?"

Ah, so *that* was what was bugging her. "I had intended to," he said, "but now that I've been accepted so well, I'm starting to rethink my original opinion."

"You are? Really?"

"Yes, I am." He paused for effect. "I have a couple of new ideas for expanding the existing downtown, or maybe adding a strip mall out near the old Randall Manufacturing plant. There's plenty of vacant land on the outskirts of town."

"Yes, there is! That's a wonderful idea."

"You can't publish any of this yet," Josh warned. "If word gets out too soon it could ruin any deals I happen to have on the table."

"But…"

He was adamant. "No buts, Whitney. Remember, you promised that if I'd tell you all my secrets you'd hold off submitting the story to your editor until I was ready."

"How much longer will that be?"

"I was originally going to wait until after I'd left town for good, assuming I revealed anything at all. Now, I think my official announcement should be made at the theater, like I suggested before."

"At least that's only a few more days."

"Right. I'm sure you can control your urge to tell all for that short a time."

"Will you be coming home before then?" she asked, sounding as if she wanted him to do so.

"I'm going to try," Josh told her, touched by her reference to *home* in connection with him. "My schedule has to remain open for the present but I promise I'll do my best to make it soon."

"I miss you," Whitney said.

The pathos in her tone was unmistakable. "I miss you, too. Hang in there. This will all work out for the best. I promise you it will."

"There you go again, telling me to hang in," she quipped. "I may have been pretty out of it after I totaled my car but

I do remember you saying that when I was literally hanging by my seat belt."

"How about when you were in the hospital?" he asked, holding his breath. "Do you remember anything that happened while you were warming up and sleeping off the effects of the accident and hypothermia?"

She sighed noisily. "Unfortunately, no. Mom asked me the same question. Was I a bad patient?"

"You could never be a bad anything," Josh told her. "If you think of any more questions you want to ask me, write them down and save them for tomorrow. I'll phone again at about the same time."

Hanging up, he prayed he was handling this situation correctly. Being a hardnosed, focused businessman was a lot easier than opening up and showing consideration, he mused. Particularly in regard to Whitney Leigh. She was as determined as ever. And he had not given her any information that wasn't completely true.

The problem was he had also not revealed everything. Not yet. He was saving some important details for the gala at the theater. At this point, his fondest wish was that Whitney would be able to accept his final surprises.

And him.

"Aargh!"

Betty heard Whitney's exclamation from the living room and hurried to see what was wrong.

She stuck her head in the doorway to her daughter's room. "Are you okay?"

"Peachy." She saved the info on her computer with a keystroke, then turned to face her mother. "Josh just phoned."

"I heard your cell. I'd hoped that was him." Studying Whitney, she scowled. "You don't look nearly as happy as I thought you would."

"He's still in St. Louis and won't commit to coming back in time to spend Christmas Day with us."

"I thought he'd explained all that. He has business to handle, doesn't he?"

"So he claims."

"You can't kid me," Betty drawled. "You believe him. You're just jealous."

"I might be if I thought he had a girlfriend up there," Whitney said. "It's not that. It's his hardheaded attitude that drives me crazy."

"You're not still holding a grudge because he fooled you so well, are you?"

"After he risked his life to pull me out of that teetering car I couldn't stay mad if I wanted to. And I don't want to. I want Josh to come home so we can talk. Really talk, not make polite conversation on a phone. I want to see his face. I need to watch his eyes so I can judge how he feels about me."

"I saw enough while you were in the hospital to tell you that," Betty said. "The poor guy is crazy about you."

"He sure has a funny way of showing it. When I woke up yesterday and saw him there, he didn't even hold my hand, let alone hug or kiss me."

"Not all men are that demonstrative," her mother warned. "He may be a genius with computers but that doesn't mean he understands what women need."

Whitney threw her hands up and made another unintelligible noise, following it with, "*He* doesn't understand? Make that two of us. I have no idea what I want. I only know that if I have to *tell* him, it won't be the same."

She wasn't pleased when her mother chuckled and shook her head. "And you expect poor Josh to figure you out when you can't decide what you want, either?"

The irony was not lost on Whitney. She, too, began to smile. "Pretty tough, huh?"

"I'd say so. Why don't you have a talk with one of your friends? How about Lily or Melissa? Or even Gracie, although I'd leave her for last if you have any choice. That poor girl was awfully mixed up for a while."

"Well, at least she was smart enough to walk away from the wrong man, even if it did make her a laughingstock. Not every bride ditches a rich groom at the altar."

"Money is no substitute for love." Betty gestured toward the laptop that still displayed a page of text. "As soon as you're done working, come and join us in the den. Dad and I are going to watch a movie I rented."

"Go ahead and start without me," Whitney said, pensive and staring at the computer screen. "I want to work on this article. It needs to be polished and ready to print before Friday night so Josh can proof it for accuracy."

"He will come back, you know. If he said he'd be here, he'll do whatever he has to in order to keep that promise."

Nodding tacit agreement, Whitney made no verbal comment. She knew in her heart that Josh wanted to return to Bygones, but what if his business needed him elsewhere? What then? And what about the future? Was this absence just a small sample of what lay ahead?

She couldn't expect Josh to abandon his lucrative career in order to make her happy, nor was she certain she'd want to leave all her friends, family and job in Bygones to go live in a big city with him.

"Besides, he hasn't asked me to," Whitney grumbled. "There's no sense imagining some rosy future with Josh Barton when he may have no such thing in mind."

Nevertheless, as soon as she got the chance, she was going to tell him how much she cared for him, even if he laughed at her. He was a much more complicated man than she'd imagined when she'd thought he was a mere shopkeeper who liked to tinker with computers.

In the back of her mind, Whitney wished she could return to the days when she was his faithful customer and he just served her coffee.

Sadly, that was never going to be possible, she admitted with a sigh. Josh was not the man she had fallen in love with.

The important question was whether the real Josh Barton was enough like the person she loved to take his place in her affections.

She hoped and prayed he was.

But she was not positive.

Not even close.

Chapter Nineteen

Christmas morning in Bygones brought clear skies and warm enough daytime temperatures that most of the lingering snow melted away.

In northeastern Missouri, however, the weather was far less accommodating.

Josh peered out his high-rise office window into the swirling snow. It was so dense he could barely make out the famous St. Louis arch in the distance.

Since time was of the essence, he'd decided to use the corporate helicopter for his return to Bygones, only now it looked as if the storm was going to prevent his doing that.

Reluctantly, he phoned Whitney. Her number went directly to voice mail.

"It's me, Josh," he said. "I hate to leave this news as a recording but I just checked and you're not online, either, so here goes. Nobody else is working today so I thought I'd..."

Beep.

Struggling to keep his temper in check, Josh redialed to continue. As soon as he heard the voice mail message end he began to talk fast.

"I got cut off. Here's the thing. It's too late to try to drive, particularly in bad weather, and flying is out, too. I was going to..."

Beep.

Frustration colored his mutterings as he tried a third time.

"Look, Whitney, the bottom line is, I'm not going to make it to your house today. I'm sorry. It can't be helped."

He had intended to add a loving holiday greeting but was once more cut off.

Before he could try again, his phone jingled with an incoming call. Thinking it was Whitney, he answered enthusiastically. "Hello!"

"Hi, honey," Susanna said. "I'm just calling to wish you a Merry Christmas."

"Hi, Mom. How's the cruise going? I never did get any emails from you while you were at sea."

"That's because I didn't go," his mother replied. "Two of my friends got sick just before we were scheduled to sail so we postponed our trip until we could all go."

"You're home?"

"Yes."

"In that case, how would you like some company? I happen to be stuck in St. Louis, at least until this storm passes."

"I'd love it! This is wonderful. We can have a nice, quiet holiday and catch up with what we've both been doing."

"You have no idea," Josh told her, smiling at the strange way his celebration of Christmas was unfolding. "I'll pick up a pizza on my way over and we can kick back together."

"A pizza? You?" Susanna giggled. "You used to be nearly as fussy about wanting fancy meals as your dad was. When did you get so normal?"

Josh had to laugh. "I'll tell you the whole story when I see you. It's long and complicated but you'll like it. I know you will."

"Anything that brings you home today suits me," his mother said. "See you soon?"

"Absolutely. I'm at the office. I sent everybody else home

early yesterday after the Christmas party when we heard a storm was coming."

"The what? Did you say you'd thrown a Christmas party? I don't believe it."

"Believe it," Josh replied with a soft chuckle. "I had it catered so there wouldn't be any question about drinks and nobody would have to prepare food at home. I wanted it to be a happy time with no requirements from any of my staff. Oh, and I handed out hefty bonuses."

"Okay," Susanna drawled. "Who are you and what have you done with my son? You're obviously an imposter."

"I'll fill you in soon," Josh said, letting his spirits soar as he thought of Whitney and the effect she and Bygones had had on his whole attitude. "And while you're waiting for me to get there, I want you to put together a list of your high school classmates, as many as you can remember. Names and addresses."

"It was a really small graduating class and I've only kept in touch with a few," Susanna said.

"That's all right. It'll do for my purposes. Email or phone those people, if you don't mind, and ask them if they're up to taking a short trip in a couple of days."

"Josh, honey, you're scaring me. I don't remember ever hearing you sound this happy. Are you sure you haven't had a nervous breakdown or something?"

"I've never been more sure of anything," he said, laughing. "Just get started calling your classmates and ask them to stand by for details. I'll explain everything when I get there."

Whitney had decided to distract herself from the disappointment of not spending Christmas with Josh by attending the special Christmas Eve service at Bygones Community Church. It hadn't helped. As much as she loved everyone there, she'd still felt Josh's absence acutely. It was as if the warmth and ambience of the familiar sanctuary had been missing something vital.

Thinking back on the service, she remembered filing out afterward with the rest of the congregation and being grateful toward God, her church, her friends and Bygones, in spite of the empty place in her life that should have been filled by the presence of the man she loved.

Did Josh care for her as much as she cared for him? she kept wondering. And if so, why had he not put his feelings into words?

"Maybe because I haven't," she muttered, surprising herself.

Really? Could she be as guilty of holding back as Josh was?

"I have good reasons," Whitney argued. "I didn't know who he really was until a few days ago. He knows exactly who I am."

Which was true—as far as she'd taken it—but it was still a pretty poor excuse. So what was holding her back?

The word *fear* popped into her head and lingered while she tried to find a suitable excuse to counter it.

There was none. She had been a coward because she hadn't wanted to risk rejection. That was precisely the reasoning her mother had given when guessing why Josh had also been uncommunicative.

Okay, Whitney decided. *What am I going to do about it?*

"Call him. Right now," she insisted, reaching for her cell phone.

There were several messages waiting in voice mail. All from Josh! Overjoyed, Whitney played them. When she got to the last one and heard his businesslike excuse and the brusque way he'd deliver it, her elation vanished.

So did her notion of phoning him to confess her love. She might be certain of her own feelings but it certainly didn't sound as if Josh shared them. No way was she going to make a fool of herself over the phone.

"Not when I can do it so much better in person," she mocked. "I will tell him how I feel. But I am not going to do it in a phone message or an email. He's going to have to tell me to my face if he's not interested in a romantic relationship."

Would face-to-face rejection hurt more? Of course it would. That didn't matter, because there was still a chance that when Josh saw the glowing affection in her expression he would understand better, perhaps even change his mind about holding back and bring himself to admit he returned her love.

Was she fooling herself? Maybe. And maybe he was every bit as introverted as her mother had guessed.

How would a man who had been raised in a home where holiday tradition was thwarted and family love was rarely expressed deal with the atmosphere in Bygones? Or in the Leigh home and their community church?

Looking at Josh's situation that way brought out Whitney's compassion and empathy. He had made great strides in the past few months. Perhaps she was expecting too much from him.

Peace filled her. She laid aside her phone. If Josh failed to arrive in the next few days, for whatever reason, she would pray hard for the wisdom and strength to forgive him again. To trust him, no matter what.

If she truly loved him, as she knew she did, there was no other option.

"I've decided to make the announcement to the entire town at once," Josh told Susanna as he concluded his story of the six months he'd spent in her old hometown. "That's why I wanted you to call your classmates. I'd like as many of them to come Friday night as possible so you can all surprise Miss Coraline. If anybody in Bygones deserves to have her wishes granted, it's that lady."

Susanna was grinning and blinking away the occasional tear. "I can hardly take all this in. You did it for me?"

"That was how it started," Josh said. "Only it sure didn't turn out the way I'd expected." He paused and cleared his throat. "Remember the nosy reporter I mentioned? Well, I have a surprise planned for her, too."

"Did you buy her a new convertible because she wrecked hers? That would make a great Christmas present."

He shook his head. "I've been so distracted lately I didn't buy her anything special for Christmas. I suppose I thought saving Bygones would be enough."

His mother was shaking her head and grimacing. "Not if you value her friendship and loyalty. After all, she is holding back her exposé for your benefit."

"True." He glanced at his Rolex, glad to have it back on his wrist now that he was no longer playing the pauper. "It's pretty late to be shopping. I imagine all the jewelry stores are closed."

"You're going to buy her jewelry?"

Josh arched an eyebrow at his mother's disparaging tone. "Why not? That's what Dad always got for you." He huffed. "You must have a fortune in expensive trinkets."

Because she was slowly shaking her head and looked so sad, he waited for her to explain further. When she didn't, he patted her hand. "What is it? What's wrong?"

"I suppose I can tell you now that your father's gone. Nearly every one of those extravagant gifts was an apology for breaking his marriage vows. I knew what was going on. If I'd had the backbone, I'd have left him long before he died."

This explained a lot. "Why didn't you?"

"Because I loved him. And I felt sorry for him. He was

never truly happy, you know. All he really cared about was making money and getting ahead in business."

Her voice faltered. Unshed tears filled her eyes. "For a long time I was afraid you were too much like him."

"Maybe in a way, I was," Josh said. "But not anymore. I think my move to Bygones was God's plan for showing me what I was missing."

By now, tears were flowing down Susanna's cheeks. As she whisked them away she stared at her only child. "God?"

"I joined the Community Church, too," Josh told her. "Pastor Garman explained everything to me and I turned my life over to the Lord."

Susanna enfolded him in a tight embrace. "That news is the best Christmas present I've ever gotten."

It seemed to Whitney that Christmas Day and the one following were the longest she had ever endured. Josh had called the Leigh house to wish her family a belated Merry Christmas on Thursday but had not said anything particularly endearing to her, other than to promise he would fly back in time for the Friday night gala in the old theater.

As she hung up the phone, she let her disgust show enough that Betty noticed. "What's the matter, Whitney? He called. And he explained again. I wouldn't want anybody to risk their life braving a storm in a helicopter just to get here on a certain date, would you?"

"He shouldn't have left in the first place."

"Why not? He had a business to run that he'd been ignoring for a long time for all our sakes."

Whitney scowled. "How did you know that?"

"I put two and two together. You already told me who he was and what he did for a living. It only stands to reason that he'd been neglecting his company. We should all appreciate his sacrifice."

"I do, I do." Whitney punctuated her comment with a

sigh. "I suppose it is selfish of me to want him to stay in Bygones when he belongs somewhere else."

"Is that what he told you?"

"He left, didn't he?"

Betty was shaking her head and beginning to smile. "Stop imagining obstructions where there are none. Josh promised to be back in time for the party and if it's humanly possible he will be." She chuckled. "I can't picture anybody commuting by helicopter, can you?"

"Unfortunately, yes," Whitney said, pulling a face. "I wouldn't be surprised to learn he has a corporate jet, too."

"You're acting like it's a crime to be successful."

Whitney rolled her eyes in frustration. "It's not that. I was just starting to believe Josh belonged here and now I can see that he doesn't. The man comes from a whole different background, not to mention the life he lives now. There's no way I can expect him to fit into my little country world, no matter how much I wish otherwise."

Betty faced her daughter and held her by the shoulders. "When you started to date I promised myself I'd never interfere, but I'm about to break that promise. If you don't give that man a chance to show you what he's made of, I'll be very disappointed."

"Oh, I'll give him a chance," Whitney vowed. "I plan to tell him I'm crazy in love with him, even if he laughs at me."

"What makes you think he might?"

She shook her head and shrugged. "Let's just say I'm having trust issues, okay? He spent six months lying to me, then admitted he hadn't intended to confess at all until after he'd left town for good. It's hard to put my full confidence in him after hearing that."

"But he did tell you in spite of everything. And you have forgiven him. I know you have."

Nodding, Whitney affirmed her mother's comment.

"Yes. I have. But part of me keeps insisting he's still too good to be true. I'm not sure how much of the person I fell in love with is the real Josh."

"Then you'll fall in love with him all over again."

"As Miss Ann Mars would say, 'From your lips to God's ears,'" Whitney whispered. "I'm out of ideas. It's all up to Him from now on."

Betty laughed and hugged her. "That's the first totally sensible thing you've said."

Chapter Twenty

The chopper's rotors beat the air as it finally lifted off from the rooftop of Barton Technologies. Josh sat in the pilot's seat. His mother was beside him wearing the passenger's headset. Once they were in the clear and headed for Bygones, he glanced at her and smiled.

"I should have taken you flying with me before," he said, relying on their radio connection to make himself heard over the roar of the engine. "Then you wouldn't be so nervous."

"Don't count on it," Susanna answered. "I've flown lots of times in commercial planes. There's no comparison."

"You just miss having all that metal around you. Look out through the plexiglass and enjoy the view."

She had to peek between her fingers because she'd covered her face with her hands during takeoff and had yet to relax. "Okay. It's pretty. Pretty scary and pretty far down."

He chuckled. "Did you manage to get commitments from some of your high school friends?"

"Yes. They were delighted to think of returning to Bygones for a belated reunion."

"Good," Josh said. He checked his heading and altimeter. "We'll be there in no time."

"I should be upset that you were that close and hardly ever came home."

"I was there for your birthday," he reminded her.

"True. Are you really going to put a new facility in Bygones?"

Josh nodded. "Looks like it. If everything works out, doing that should finish the job of bringing back prosperity, particularly since I'm planning to pay my current staff to relocate there as well as adding local workers."

"What about you?" Susanna asked. "Are you going to live there, too? Because if you are, so am I."

"I hope to." Josh sobered. "At this point, there's only one person who could change my mind."

Whitney had spent quiet Christmastime days with her parents, using as many of her spare hours as possible to deliver token gifts and plates of food to others, such as Miss Ann Mars who lived above the This 'N' That.

The white-haired octogenarian had been clearly delighted to welcome a visitor. "Whitney! Come in, come in. I was just enjoying a cup of tea. Will you join me?"

"That sounds nice," Whitney had said, holding out the covered plate. "Mom sent you some ham and other fixings, just in case you hadn't bothered with a big meal."

"Aren't you sweet?" The spry but bent little old woman led the way into her kitchenette. "Just put that on the table, dear. I'll boil more water for our tea. And help yourself to some sweets if you like. As you can see, a lot of my friends treated me."

"You deserve every cookie," Whitney said, admiring the homemade assortments. "You do so much for all of us. Like providing those outdoor Christmas decorations, for instance."

"Nonsense. I just share what the good Lord gives me."

Whitney sank into a chair at the small kitchen table,

shed her coat and propped her elbows on the red-and-white-checkered cloth. "Have you ever wondered what you'd do if you suddenly had a lot more money?"

Ann giggled like a nervous teenager. "Mercy me. What makes you ask that?"

"Just wondering. About a lot of things," Whitney told her solemnly.

Waiting for the water to boil, Miss Ann joined her guest at the table and set a cup with a teabag in front of her. "I didn't think there was anyone left who remembered."

"Remembered what?"

"My youth." She began to smile as if she were reliving a happy, carefree time. "I was quite a catch in those days, you know. The fellas were all chasing me."

"But you never married?"

Ann shook her head and tucked stray white strands back into the customary bun at her nape. "I came close. Once. If my daddy hadn't interfered I might have been Dale Eversleigh's grandma."

Whitney almost choked on a bite of sugar cookie. "You what? How?"

"His granddaddy came courtin' me, long ago. We were in love, or at least we thought we were. But my papa didn't think the boy had enough promise and he didn't cotton to my living behind a funeral parlor, either, so we broke up."

"Is that why you stayed single?"

"Maybe. It's hard to remember. Then, of course, my former beau went on to make a success of his business and leave quite a legacy to be passed down to Dale." She lost her wistfulness and began to smile again. "The boy'd be a whole lot more good-looking if I'd birthed his daddy, I'll tell you. I want to laugh every time I see him flash that gold tooth of his."

Whitney was shaking her head in astonishment. "How

many other wonderful stories are you keeping to yourself, Miss Ann?"

"Probably more than it's wise to air," the elderly woman said with a wink. "So, tell me, how is your love life these days? Are you and Josh Smith really a couple?"

"Word travels fast."

"Fast, but not necessarily true. I'd like to hear the whole thing from you, dear. Has he popped the question yet?"

"He hasn't even told me he loves me."

"Ah. Well, in my day we weren't quite so outspoken. If a boy wanted to court me he didn't hug me out in the street in front of a whole passel of folks. He might not even hold my hand until he was ready to get real serious."

"I suppose you mean what happened when Josh and I were helping the volunteers decorate."

"Mmm-hmm." She poured hot water into Whitney's cup. "I also heard that you wrecked that cute little car of yours. What a shame. Is it a total loss?"

"Fortunately, no," Whitney reported. "I'll need a new top and work done on the windows, but the metal wasn't badly bent because it landed in snow, I guess."

"That's good. Word is that a certain handsome man came to your rescue."

"Yes." Whitney sighed. "It was amazing. Josh was out looking for me after we'd had a misunderstanding. He got his van stuck and when he called Elwood to tow him, they discovered me. I was trapped in my car. I don't think I've ever been that cold before."

"Sounds like a Christmas present of sorts."

"Really?"

"Yes. From the good Lord." Ann paused to sip from her own cup. "Don't make the same mistake I did and let the right man get away, Whitney. It's too late for me to change my life but hopefully you can benefit from the mess I let my daddy make of mine." She stared into the distance as if seeing something that wasn't there. "If I'd known then what I know now, I'd have defied my father and married the man I loved."

"My parents like Josh," Whitney admitted ruefully. "The problem is not from outside forces being against us, it's all me. I'm having trouble adjusting to the fact that he fooled me so completely."

Ann scowled. "He did? How? When?"

"Oops. I've said too much." She pushed away from the table and stood. "There's going to be a big bash at the old theater on Friday night. If you want to hear the whole story, you need to be there at six, sharp. Can you get a ride or do you want me to come pick you up?"

"I'll have Danny Wilbur or his daddy, Kenneth, drive me over. In the meantime, why don't you take some of these cookies with you? I have way more than I can eat."

"You keep them. They'll freeze nicely," Whitney told her. "Enjoy your meal."

"Tell your mother thanks for me," Ann said. She followed Whitney to the door. "Are you sure you don't want to tell me more? You wouldn't want to be responsible for causing a sweet innocent old lady to die of curiosity, would you?"

That ridiculous comment had made Whitney laugh. She'd gently hugged Ann. "You may be old and sweet, but you're far from innocent. Have a lovely dinner and I'll see you at the movies."

"Will your young man be there?"

"I certainly hope so," Whitney had told her. "Since he's the one who's throwing the party."

Josh had arranged for Coraline to pick them up as soon as they arrived in Bygones. Landing in the parking lot of the former Randall plant, Josh helped his mother disembark, then stood back while the women held a tearful reunion.

Robert Randall had chauffeured Coraline.

Josh joined him and they shook hands. "Merry Christmas."

"I sure hope so." Randall's questioning look focused on the closed building behind them. "I know it's early yet but I wondered…"

"Looks like a done deal," Josh told him. "Once my attorneys finish the paperwork and we both sign off on the terms of the sale, we'll be good to go. Have you thought over my suggestion? I will need a local consultant, even after we hire a full staff."

"I've thought about it." Grinning, Randall nodded toward Coraline and Susanna. "If I agree, I'm going to need time off for a honeymoon. I assume that can be arranged."

Josh clapped him on the shoulder and vigorously pumped his hand again. "Congratulations, you old dog. I'm glad to see you finally came to your senses. Miss Coraline is a fine woman."

"There's another equally perfect, single girl around, you know. Have you decided what to do about Whitney?"

"I have. I really blew it when I came to town in disguise."

"Yes, but you had good reasons, according to my future bride. So, what's next?"

"The movie and announcements tonight. You'll be there, of course."

"Wouldn't miss it," Robert said, eyeing the teary reunion between Coraline and Susanna. "Where is your mother going to stay while she's in town?"

"I hadn't thought about that," Josh admitted. "Any ideas?"

"Sure. I can take Coraline's sons to my house with me and leave her house for all the women. It'll be just her, your mother and Coraline's daughter, Cindy."

"Sounds great. Thanks. I have a lot to arrange before tonight and Mom needs to catch up on local news, anyway."

"Have you told her about Whitney?"

"You mean have I warned her?"

"Something like that. There was a nice article in the last *Gazette* about the reopening of the theater. Are you really inviting the whole town?"

"As many as we can squeeze in, with overflow in the lobby if necessary," Josh said. "I've redone the projection system in digital format to keep up with technological advances. I'm not sure whether I'll operate the theater all the time or just keep it for special occasions. A lot will depend on how many of your former employees choose to come back to Bygones and start living here again."

"I have one man I can suggest already," Robert said. "Brian Montclair is an excellent manager. He'd be an asset to Barton Technologies."

"Do you think he'd consider leaving the bakery?"

Robert laughed again. "For a job that doesn't require him to wear an apron? That's a no-brainer."

"All right. After I make the initial statements at the theater, I'll tell anyone who's interested in a possible job to see you and put their name on a waiting list." Josh raised his hand as if bestowing knighthood on Robert. "I hereby dub you official personnel director—with time off for your honeymoon, of course."

Randall grasped Josh's hand and shook it again, capping their clasped fingers with his free hand. "I don't care what name you use or anything else about you. You're okay in my book. Very okay."

"Thanks," Josh said, touched by the candor and show of friendship. "I hope you're not the only one who thinks so after tonight."

"What's next for you?" Robert asked. "Would you like to join us for an early dinner?"

"I'll take a rain check this time," Josh said pleasantly. "I've already arranged with Melissa at Sweet Dreams and

Elwood at The Everything to provide refreshments for tonight, but I have to pick up a few personal items first. Do you think Miss Ann will open the This 'N' That for me, even if it's closed for the holidays?"

Robert looked puzzled. "I'm sure she will. What in the world do you need from that place?"

"It's a secret." Josh couldn't help grinning. He'd had a brainstorm on his way to Bygones and was only one more step away from implementing it.

Yes, it was chancy. But it was also the perfect way to approach Whitney and prove he was her kind of guy. He hoped. Time would tell. He could hardly wait.

Whitney had heard rumors about Josh's impressive arrival before he phoned her.

"I needed to get my mother settled at Coraline's," he explained.

"Your mother is here? In Bygones? Now?"

"Yes. I told you she was born and raised here."

Did you bring her here to meet me? Whitney wondered, feeling her hopes soar.

Instead of voicing that, she asked, "Did you get the text file I emailed? That's the final version of my article unless you can think of something else."

"It's fine. Are you all set to print it?"

"Yes. Ed knows to reserve empty space on the front page for a picture and my big news. I've told him it's going to knock his socks off and he believed me enough to agree to hold the presses."

"Wonderful. I'd offer to pick you up if I had wheels."

"I heard about your mind-boggling arrival. Flying in aboard your own helicopter is hardly the best way to maintain your pose as a simple shopkeeper."

"That won't last long, anyway," Josh said. "And I was

afraid bad road conditions might make me late. I'd promised you I'd be here, and here I am."

You certainly are, Whitney thought, cradling the phone. "So, what's plan A?"

"I figured to put out the hot food after the film. Melissa's cookies will be served with cider and tea before my announcement. We'll do that, run the movie, then Velma and Elwood will man the snack booth."

"Okay. I'll bring my laptop and be ready to transmit my scoop to the *Gazette* as soon as you give the word."

"Fair enough. We can use the Wi-Fi from the Cozy Cup." He paused. Cleared his throat. "Thank you, Whitney. I really appreciate your consideration."

"As long as I get my story filed ASAP I'll be happy."

"I want you to meet me on stage, behind the curtain," Josh said. "I'd like you there when I make the big announcement."

"Why? What can I do?"

"Offer moral support if nothing else," he said. "I know you were pretty steamed when you found out the truth about me and I'd like some company if I end up ducking rotten tomatoes."

"They're out of season," she said, stifling a laugh. "But look out for snowballs."

"Thanks for the tip. You will stand with me and watch my back, won't you?"

"Yes," she said, wondering if he was half as eager to see her again as she was to be with him.

The simple fact that he had requested her presence on the stage beside him was *almost* enough to convince her everything was going to be okay.

Chapter Twenty-One

Josh patted his jacket pocket to assure himself he still had the special surprise item he needed. The crowd entering the old theater had filled nearly every seat except the two he'd reserved on the main aisle in the very last row for himself and Whitney.

Townspeople were conversing so boisterously the whole place buzzed and hummed.

Red velvet curtains separated him from the audience. He checked his watch and peeked out. Almost time. Where was Whitney? If she didn't show up, all his perfect plans would be for nothing.

"Hey!" she called, rushing in from the rear alley instead of fighting through the crowd out front.

Josh whirled, grinning so broadly he was certain she could tell how glad he was to see her. "You came!" He reached to help her off with her coat.

"I promised I would, didn't I?"

"Sorry I didn't make it back for Christmas. I meant to. If the weather had cooperated I'd have been here. You know I would."

"I know."

Judging by the way her expression softened and her

cheeks grew rosier, she looked as though she actually believed him. That was certainly a step in the right direction.

Josh reached for her hand and held it gently. "I like that red sweater. And leaving your hair down, too. If you get any prettier I won't know how to act."

"Just be yourself," Whitney said, focusing on his eyes and staring into them as if trying to glimpse his innermost thoughts.

His fingers tightened around hers and he gestured at the split in the heavy curtain. "That's exactly what I plan to do. Are you ready?"

"As ready as I'll ever be," Whitney said, tossing her head to flip back her long, blond hair. "Let's get this over with before I lose my nerve."

Josh pulled back the curtain just enough for them to step through. If Whitney had not been holding his hand she might have balked at the size of the gathering. Every soul in Bygones must be out there. People were crammed into the seats while the overflow crowd stood in the back and lined the outer aisles against the soundproofed walls.

She and Josh were greeted by a hush of conversation and a smattering of applause. When he raised a hand to wave, so did she.

An old-fashioned microphone waited atop a metal stand in the center of the narrow stage apron.

Josh led her to it and began to speak. As expected, he first introduced himself by his real name.

"Those of you who know me as Josh Smith may be surprised to learn that my last name is actually Barton, although anybody who read the logo on the side of my helicopter has probably figured that out."

There was an undercurrent of laughter in the crowd, along with a few louder exclamations. *So far, so good,* Whitney thought, wondering how he could sound so calm when she was a nervous as a kitten locked in a pen with a bunch of unfriendly stray dogs.

"I'll fill you all in on the entire story in a minute," Josh told his audience. "But first, I have something else to do. Something very important, as you'll soon see."

Whitney frowned. She watched him step back and reach into his jacket pocket. What he pulled out was made of gold-colored plastic with a cloudy glob of glass mounted in the center. Her mouth dropped open as she recognized one of the mood rings from Miss Ann's store.

There was a twinkle in Josh's eyes as he dropped to one knee and offered the ring as if it were an exquisite diamond.

Smiling, he said, "Whitney Leigh, I love you. Will you marry me?"

No one breathed. Especially not Whitney. Not only was he asking her to marry him, he was doing it in front of hundreds of witnesses.

Words failed her. She merely nodded.

Josh stood and slipped the toy ring on her finger. Leaning closer so the microphone wouldn't pick up his voice he said, "I didn't want you to think I was putting on airs so I got you an inexpensive engagement ring right here in Bygones. I hope you like it."

Happier than she had ever been and surer of her future than even her fondest dreams had predicted, she threw her arms around Josh's neck and kissed him.

Below them on the main floor of the theater, the townspeople began to cheer.

It took several minutes for the crowd to quiet down but that was fine with Whitney. She put the time to good use by kissing her future husband. More than once.

Josh finally came up for air and gently set her away before facing the mic again. "Whew! That was the tricky part. Now for the rest of the story," he said with a face-splitting grin.

"I'd intended to ride off into the sunset without telling anybody who I am, but Whitney made me change my mind." He cleared his throat. "She is one determined lady, as all of you undoubtedly know."

A few laughs came from the audience but most were quiet, hanging on his every word and increasing his concern that their warm welcome might be withdrawn at any moment.

"That's why I'm standing up here tonight. I'm not looking for praise or thanks, I'm asking you all to forgive me for deceiving you by pretending to be Josh Smith instead of using my real name. At the time, it seemed like the sensible thing to do. Now I can see it was a mistake to hide my efforts to help put Bygones back on its feet."

Murmuring increased to a low hum.

Josh grasped the mic stand and pressed on. "The original grants for the Save Our Streets project came from me. In the beginning I acted because of my mother, the former Susanna Hastings. I'm sure a lot of you old-timers remember her and her folks. Anyway, she was heartbroken when Miss Coraline had to cancel the reunion. That's what started me thinking about ways to help her favorite old town. The rest you know. I set up a dummy corporation and went to work here, myself, to make sure my plans were carried out."

He grinned down at the audience as he reached for Whitney's hand once more. "I'm happy to report everything turned out a lot better than even I had imagined."

A few people started to clap for him. Josh held up his free hand to ask for quiet. "One more thing before we start the film. I liked living here so much I've decided to make a permanent move—for me and for Barton Technologies. All the papers are not yet signed but I think it's safe to say the deal is going to go through. There will be a new company in town to offer more local jobs, as well as maybe more commerce when I get around to implementing other plans. It won't be fast, but it is coming. I'll see to it."

This time, he stood back and accepted the loud applause and hoots of joy before adding, "You all know Robert Randall. He'll be available after the movie when we have our supper out in the lobby. If you're interested in applying for a job, be sure to see him."

Josh stepped back, taking Whitney with him, and they ducked through the velvet curtains before he once again embraced her.

"No rotten tomatoes or snowballs," he said, smiling.

Whitney giggled and kissed him soundly before she teased, "The night is young."

A few minutes later, Whitney and Josh each pulled out personal computers backstage. She sent her exclusive to the *Gazette* via hers, while he activated the program that would dim the house lights and show the classic film in digital form.

Whitney looked down at the silly plastic ring on her left hand. Josh had promised her a real diamond and she was certain he'd keep his word. But no matter how much luxurious jewelry he bought for her, she would always treasure this token of his love. It was positive proof that he understood her, that he accepted her quirks just as she accepted his.

"Okay, mission accomplished," she said. "Shall we join the others to watch the movie?"

"If we have to," he drawled. "Personally, I kind of like the privacy back here."

Blushing, she took a playful swat at his shoulder. "In that case, I *know* we'd better go out front."

As they took their reserved seats, Whitney noticed Robert and Coraline in the row directly ahead of them.

Whitney saw him lean closer to whisper in Coraline's ear and watched as the older couple kissed.

"I think we've started something," Josh said softly as he slipped his arm around Whitney's shoulders.

"More like we've ended it," she quipped. "You were the last newcomer to fall in love."

"So far," he said with a nod. "I plan to build a strip mall near the new Barton plant and encourage plenty of my original employees to relocate to Bygones. Plus, there'll be enough funding to keep the schools open and reinstate the police officers who were laid off, so you'd better keep your pencil sharpened. There's no telling what will happen when I bring all that new blood into this sleepy little town."

"As long as you don't leave, I don't care," Whitney said, cuddling closer. "I've never been happier than I am right now." She was absently fiddling with the loose ring.

"Even after I bought your engagement ring at the This 'N' That?"

"Especially then," Whitney said, grinning. "You are the coolest rich guy I've ever met."

"How many of them do you know?" Josh asked, echoing his quip about her being his favorite reporter.

"One," Whitney said with a grin. "And one is quite enough."

Epilogue

Christmas was a distant memory by the time Whitney's mother joined her in an anteroom of the Community Church.

"You're a beautiful bride," Betty said with a sigh. "I'm so glad you decided to wear the wedding dress I saved all these years."

"So am I. I just wish I wasn't so nervous. I can hardly think straight," Whitney confessed. "Writing about Allison and Sam's wedding last week was a lot easier than walking down the aisle myself is going to be."

"Your dad will keep you from falling on your face," Betty joked. "Of maybe you're the one who will have to hold him up."

"I sure hope not. Have you seen Josh?"

"Yes, and he's the handsomest guy in the building." She laughed. "Except maybe for J.T. He cleans up really well. I'm glad you waited until he didn't need a cane anymore."

"It wasn't my idea," Whitney confessed. "Josh had some crazy idea that I wouldn't be happy unless we had a big wedding."

"Uh-oh."

"What?" Whitney held her breath. "Don't tell me he's been keeping more secrets."

"No, no." Her mother waved her hands and shook her head so hard Whitney expected her tiny hat to slip. "It's my fault. And Susanna's. We were the ones who convinced him you needed a fancy shindig so everybody in Bygones could share the moment."

"Mom! You didn't."

"Afraid we did. It's a good thing you and Josh never compared notes about it or we wouldn't be standing here right now."

"We sure wouldn't." Astounded but too happy to argue at this late date, Whitney headed for the door to the sanctuary as the music began to swell.

Like the theater had been six months before, the church was packed to the walls with stragglers extending onto the foyer and out the door. Lily Bronson, formerly Farnsworth, her matron of honor and the provider of all the gorgeous flowers, was waiting to hand Whitney her bridal bouquet.

Melissa Montclair, née Sweeney, dashed up at the last minute to take her place as one of the bridesmaids. "The cake's fine. Brian put the finishing touches on it without getting frosting on his tux," she said breathlessly.

Whitney smiled over at Gracie Fogerty, delighted that she and her Patrick had finally tied the knot, too. Allison and Sam Franklin were away on their honeymoon but Vivian Duncan had agreed to become the fourth attendant. Asking Tate, Brian, Patrick and Chase Rollins, who was currently engaged to Vivian, to stand up with Josh had made perfect sense and had pleased everyone.

Whitney watched the other lovely women precede her down the aisle, their pastel dresses reminding her of the bright spring flowers that accented their ensembles.

Then, it was her turn. Taking her father's arm, she smiled at her waiting groom.

"Mom was right," she crooned. "Josh looks amazing."

"So does my little girl," J.T. told her. "That lacy dress of your mother's is still a knockout. Ready?"

Whitney nodded.

The aisle seemed miles long, yet she finally reached Josh and took his hand as her father gave the appropriate response to, "Who gives this woman?"

"I have a secret almost as good as yours was," she whispered to her future husband. "It was our mothers who wanted this big wedding, not me."

His astonished expression almost made her laugh.

"You're kidding!"

"Nope. Scout's honor."

"Want to elope?" Josh asked, grinning conspiratorially.

"I'm afraid it's too late for that," Whitney said, smiling at him and loving him more than ever as they took their place in front of Pastor Garman. "We've been thoroughly bamboozled."

"I could have sworn this was your idea."

"And I thought it was yours." This time she did chuckle softly. "From now on, we need to promise to talk more."

"We'll have the rest of our lives to catch up," Josh told her. "Starting today."

In spite of being a professional writer who was already becoming known for her syndicated, folksy columns about small town life, Whitney knew she could not have said it better.

* * * * *

Dear Reader,

When I was offered this assignment by Love Inspired I was astounded since I, like Josh, have had family difficulties and conflicts regarding Christmas. But God had a lesson in mind—for me. As I wrote, I learned that some “traditions” are best left behind and new ones made, particularly when we celebrate the birth of our Lord and Savior.

Special thanks to my fellow continuity authors; Arlene James, Carolyne Aarsen, Brenda Minton, Lissa Manley and Charlotte Carter. You’ll find the list of all the series titles here, in this book.

May your faith grow daily and may you be blessed this Christmas season by the One who offers healing and forgiveness to all who believe.

Blessings,

Valerie

DISCUSSION QUESTIONS

1. As you've read each book in this series, have you felt closer and closer to the people of Bygones? How?

2. Do you think Josh did the right thing by keeping his identity a secret? Was it logical to do so?

3. Can you understand why Whitney was so determined to learn the truth? Was it just because of her job?

4. When Josh starts getting involved in volunteer work, even before this book begins, can you understand how it might affect him when he's accepted as a friend?

5. If Whitney had learned who Josh really was earlier, do you think she would have fallen in love with him? Why or why not?

6. After Whitney discovers Josh's secret, she has trouble forgiving him for lying. Is that a normal reaction?

7. As Christians, we're taught to forgive even our enemies. Is it sometimes harder to forgive a friend?

8. Whitney loves Josh. What stops her from confessing her feelings? Could it be pride?

9. When Josh becomes a Christian he learns more and more as time passes. Isn't that common? What if God dumped it all on him—or us—at once? Wouldn't that be scary?

10. Several older women, as well as men, are the glue that holds Bygones together even after commerce fades. Do you know people in your town who do the same?

11. Whitney's rescue is the result of other circumstances that come together for her benefit and as the result of Josh's prayers. Do you think we often miss this kind of divine intervention in our lives because it isn't so dramatic?

12. At the end, when Josh finally proposes, he gives Whitney a special ring. Would you accept a token like that, offered in the spirit of fun, or would it disappoint you? Why or why not?

13. Have you ever wondered if more money would make you happy? Once our basic needs are met, do we need more?

14. How about inner peace and joy? Is it dependent upon outside circumstances the way Whitney first thought, or is it provided by trusting the Lord no matter what happens? Why is that sometimes so hard to do, even for believers? Proverbs 3:5

15. Love Inspired books are special to me, as an author. How have they blessed you? Can you see how even the most dedicated Christian sometimes needs to learn something new? I certainly do!

COMING NEXT MONTH FROM
Love Inspired®

Available December 17, 2013

HER UNEXPECTED COWBOY
Cowboys of Sunrise Ranch
Debra Clopton

Determined never to fall in love, the last thing Rowdy McDermott expects is for spunky artist Lucy Calvert to literally land in his arms and into his heart.

BAYOU SWEETHEART
Lenora Worth

A troubled past has hardened millionaire Tomas Delacorte, but when he hires the bubbly Callie Moreau as his landscaper, she'll show him a world full of light and love.

HIS IDEAL MATCH
Chatam House
Arlene James

Widow Carissa Hopper thinks Phillip Chatam is bad news, but when the charming adventurer starts growing roots, can she trust that he'll stick around for her and her children?

THE FIREFIGHTER'S NEW FAMILY
Gail Gaymer Martin

Firefighter Devon Murphy risks his life daily, but when he starts to fall for widow Ashley Kern and her adorable son, he's not sure he can place his heart in the same danger.

THE RANCHER'S SECRET SON
Betsy St. Amant

Emma Shaver has kept their son a mystery for years, but when she's reunited with Max Ringgold, she'll realize she can't keep her secrets—or her heart—hidden any longer.

SEASON OF REDEMPTION
Jenna Mindel

Working together on a community project will teach Ryan Marsh and Kellie Cavanaugh that sometimes the path to healing can also be the path to love.

LOOK FOR THESE AND OTHER LOVE INSPIRED BOOKS WHEREVER BOOKS ARE SOLD, INCLUDING MOST BOOKSTORES, SUPERMARKETS, DISCOUNT STORES AND DRUGSTORES.

LICNM1213